MELODY

1964

Never Stop Singing

By Denise Lewis Patrick

American Girl®

A Peek into
Melody's World
Detroit, Michigan
Big Momma's House
Our Church
Seward Ave.
My School
Duffield Library
Linwood St.
14th St.
Poppa's Flower Shop
Frank's Flo

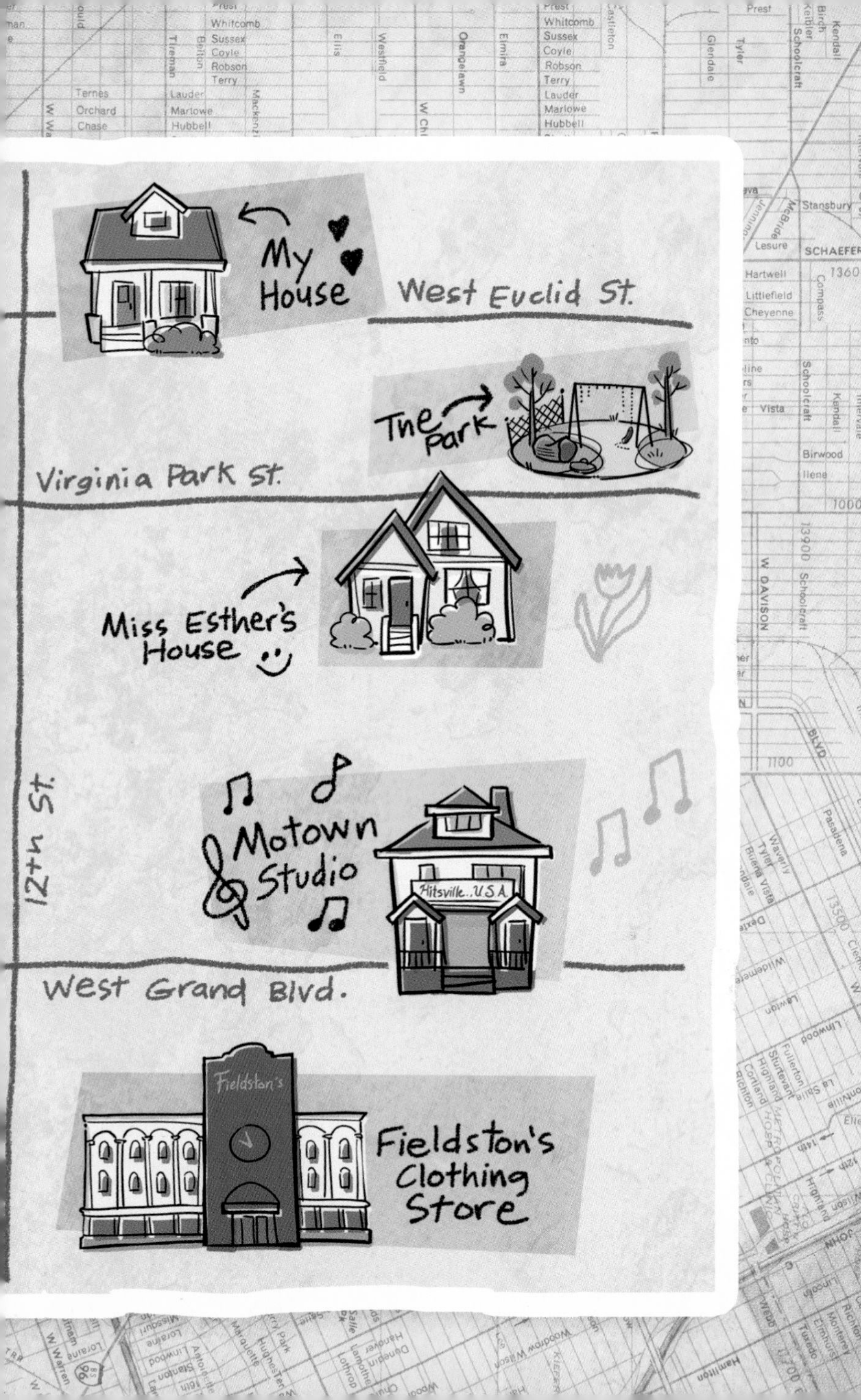

My House
West Euclid St.
The Park
Virginia Park St.
Miss Esther's House
Motown Studio
Hitsville..U.S.A.
12th St.
West Grand Blvd.
Fieldston's
Fieldston's Clothing Store

Melody's Family and Friends

Daddy and Mommy
Melody's parents

Yvonne, Lila, and Dwayne
Melody's sisters and brother

Big Momma
Melody's grandmother

Poppa
Melody's grandfather

Tish and Charles

Val's parents. Charles is Mommy's cousin.

Val

Melody's favorite cousin

Sharon

Melody's best friend

Bo

The family dog

Miss Esther

A neighbor and a member of Melody's church

Miss Dorothy

The children's choir director at church and Big Momma's best friend

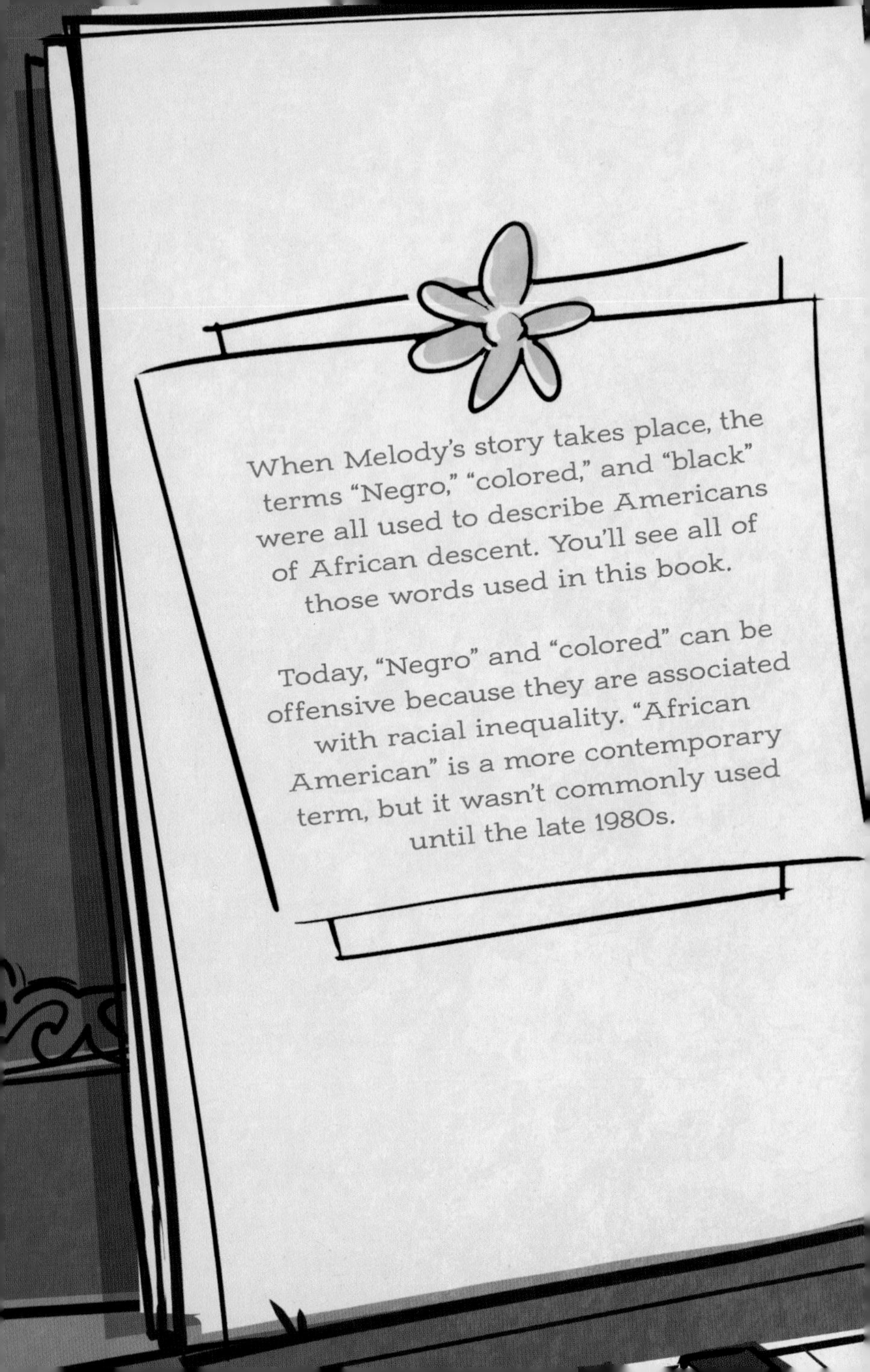
When Melody's story takes place, the terms "Negro," "colored," and "black" were all used to describe Americans of African descent. You'll see all of those words used in this book.
Today, "Negro" and "colored" can be offensive because they are associated with racial inequality. "African American" is a more contemporary term, but it wasn't commonly used until the late 1980s.

Table of Contents

Janua

Melody's Eve

CHAPTER 1

Melody Ellison stared for a moment at the bright new calendar in her hands before she put it up on the kitchen wall. The picture on the January page showed a tall evergreen tree, its thick branches frosted with snow.

"O Christmas tree, O Christmas tree, how lovely are your branches," Melody sang, even though Christmas had been over for a week. It was New Year's Eve, and tomorrow would be the first day of 1964, her tenth birthday!

Melody loved the idea that having a New Year's birthday meant that the whole world was having a birthday, too. Until now she'd been too young to stay awake past midnight, or to attend the special Watch Night service at their church. Now that she was turning ten, her parents had decided that she was old enough to do both.

Melody's sister Lila came into the kitchen with Bo, the family's mixed terrier. Lila playfully tugged at one of Melody's braids. "Dee-Dee's almost double digits!"

"That's right!" Melody said proudly. Lila was already thirteen, and Melody felt as if she was finally catching up.

"Good morning, Melody," her mother said, joining

the girls in the kitchen. "I see you're carrying on your calendar-changing tradition!"

"Yes, I am, Mommy," Melody said, watching her mother tie on a colorful apron. "And if I weren't going to help Poppa decorate the church hall for tonight, I'd help you and Lila make the cake."

"Hey! You can't help make your own birthday cake!" Lila said, taking eggs out of the refrigerator.

Mommy shook her head as she took the large mixing bowl out of the cupboard. "My baby girl is going to be ten tomorrow! Seems like it was just yesterday that you were born."

"Mommy, I'm not a baby anymore," Melody reminded her, skipping out to the living room. "I'm about to become double digits, remember?"

Melody glanced at the sunburst clock over the sofa. Her grandparents, Poppa and Big Momma, wouldn't be arriving for another half hour. So Melody turned on the TV and waited while it warmed up. When the picture appeared, she turned the knob through all the channels, looking for something fun to watch. But every station seemed to be running a program that looked back on the year's news. Melody didn't really want to be reminded. She reached for the knob to shut off the TV.

"Wait, Dee-Dee!" Melody's other sister, Yvonne, called

out from the stairs. "Don't turn it off. I want to watch."

Yvonne was home from college for the holidays, and Melody was glad to have her back for a few weeks. Now, if only their brother, Dwayne, were here! This was the first Christmas he'd ever been away, and Melody really missed him. He and his singing group, The Three Ravens, were traveling around the country singing for Motown, the famous record company. Dwayne was a talented musician, but Daddy didn't like his new career one bit. Dwayne was only eighteen, and Daddy and Mommy wanted him to go to college instead.

Melody and Yvonne sat on the sofa and watched a grainy replay of the new president, Lyndon B. Johnson, being sworn into office back in November.

Yvonne shook her head. "I still can't believe somebody killed the president of the United States," she said, turning up the sound. They listened as the grim-faced newscaster told the whole story again: how President John F. Kennedy and the First Lady were in a motorcade in Dallas, Texas, on November 22. They were riding in the back of a Lincoln Continental convertible when a man with a gun fired at them and assassinated the president.

"The country remains in shock as our new president faces a grieving nation, problems overseas, and growing civil rights protests here at home," said the newscaster.

Then he began to talk about the bombing of a Birmingham, Alabama, church that had killed four little girls. Melody turned away from the TV screen. Somebody who wanted to frighten black people away from fighting for equal rights had set off the bomb on a Sunday morning in September.

Although it had happened hundreds of miles away from Detroit, Melody had been frightened—so much so that she'd lost her voice right before the big Youth Day concert at church. For a long while she'd been afraid to go inside her own church. Her family and friends had helped her find courage, and her voice, again, but the thought of the bombing still scared Melody.

"I'll never forget that day," Yvonne said, interrupting Melody's memories.

Yvonne had been away at Tuskegee, her college, when the bombing had happened. Tuskegee was also in Alabama—only a few hours' drive from Birmingham.

"Vonnie," Melody suddenly asked, "were *you* scared?" Melody had never considered that her brave big sister might have been frightened, too.

"Yes, at first," Yvonne said. "I had signed up to go to Birmingham the very next weekend. We were going to sit at a lunch counter to protest the fact that the place refused to serve black people. But after that Sunday I wasn't sure if I should go."

Melody got up, turned the TV off, and turned back to her sister. "But you did go to Birmingham, didn't you?"

Yvonne nodded. "I remembered Mom telling me that I should always stand up to wrong. Bombing that church was wrong. Treating black people unfairly is wrong. So I decided that I had to go to Birmingham and support what I believe in, you know?"

Melody nodded. "Big Momma told me something like that, too! She said we should keep our hearts and voices strong when bad things happen. I tried really hard to be strong for the little girls in Birmingham. I *wanted* to be, only I wasn't sure I could."

Yvonne got up and gave Melody a hug. "You didn't let fear turn you around," she said. "You went back to church to sing. You *were* strong."

Melody didn't say anything. She just leaned into her sister's hug.

Just then there was a knock on the front door. Yvonne answered it, and their grandfather came in, along with a blast of cold air.

"Happy Melody's Eve, everybody!" Poppa's voice boomed. It was his joke to call New Year's Eve "Melody's Eve." Melody hurried to give him a hug.

"Are you ready to be my helper in getting the church decorated for tonight?" Poppa asked.

"Of course," Melody answered, grabbing her jacket. "Bye, Yvonne. Bye, Mommy," she called.

"Good-bye," Mommy called back. "Go make our New Hope church beautiful for tonight."

Poppa's truck was in the driveway. The words "Frank's Flowers" were on the passenger door. Poppa owned a flower shop on 12th Street, and he had taught Melody everything she knew about plants and gardening.

"Are you excited about your first Watch Night service?" Poppa asked as they climbed into the truck. "You know it's a tradition for many colored folks, especially those of us with family in the South."

Melody knew from her brother and sisters that Watch Night wouldn't exactly be a New Year's Eve party like the ones that were on TV. But there would be singing, and preaching by Pastor Daniels, with food and fellowship afterward in the church hall.

"I'm glad I can finally stay up with everybody else till midnight," she told him. "But why is it called 'Watch Night'?"

"It goes back one hundred years," Poppa explained, "to when word got out that President Abraham Lincoln planned to announce to the country that all slaves were free. The president was going to make the announcement on New Year's Day, 1863. So colored people, slave and free, sat up all night, keeping watch for freedom—Watch Night."

"But you can't *see* freedom," Melody said.

"Are you sure about that?" Poppa asked.

Melody wondered for a moment what freedom might look like. Would it look like the thousands of people who had marched in Washington, D.C., last August? Yvonne had gone to that march, and Melody and her family had watched it on TV.

"Would freedom look like people of all races doing things together?" she asked.

"Maybe," Poppa said. "Back in 1863, *that* kind of freedom was just a dream."

Melody nodded. She thought about Dr. Martin Luther King Jr., who spoke at the march in Washington. He talked about his dream.

"I think on that first Watch Night, they could see freedom coming," Poppa went on. "How many times have you tried to stay awake on Melody's Eve, because what's coming is so special? When you're expecting something big, something wonderful to happen, you can't rest. And when that Emancipation Proclamation did come, our people celebrated. We've been giving thanks ever since, during Watch Night."

Melody smiled. She was thankful that she was finally going to stay up for Watch Night. And she was proud that her birthday was linked to such an important tradition.

Watch Night

CHAPTER 2

At eleven thirty that night, Melody walked into New Hope Baptist Church and settled into her seat between Lila and Yvonne. She had sat between her sisters ever since she was a tiny girl. Now, half an hour away from turning ten, Melody felt very grown-up.

She inhaled the spicy smell of the pine branches she and Poppa had woven into a garland across the choir stand up front. As she watched for Poppa and Big Momma and her cousins to arrive, Melody looked around at everything else that was so familiar: the beautiful stained-glass windows, the worn wooden pews, the many faces she'd known forever. This church had always been her home away from home. There had been a time, right after the church bombing in Birmingham, when being here had frightened her, but now New Hope made Melody feel safe again.

When the rest of the family arrived, their cousin Val squeezed in between Melody and Lila. "It's your first Watch Night!" Val whispered. "And it's almost your birthday!"

Melody grinned. "I'm glad you're here." Val and her

parents, Charles and Tish, had moved to Detroit from Birmingham in May and were staying with Poppa and Big Momma.

Before Val could say anything else, Pastor Daniels stepped up to the pulpit.

"Good evening!" the preacher said. His voice was always loud and clear, and he never needed to use a microphone.

"Good evening!" everyone answered together.

Pastor Daniels peered out at the crowd over the tops of his glasses. "A week ago, many of us received gifts," he began. "Isn't that right?"

"Yes, sir!" a young voice answered from the back. A few people laughed, and Melody turned to look.

Pastor Daniels chuckled before he continued. "Well, New Hope church family, at midnight everyone here will receive another gift. When the New Year comes in, each of us will receive a new opportunity to make a difference in the world. And I want each one of you to ask yourself: What will *I* do to help justice, equality, and dignity grow in our community?"

Melody sat up a little straighter. She thought of the seeds she and Poppa planted in their gardens every spring and of the work it took to make those seeds grow and blossom. *Can a person really make justice, equality, and dignity grow, too?* she wondered. *How?*

Pastor Daniels kept speaking. "In honor of all those hopeful souls who first sat watch for their freedom so long ago, now is the time for every one of us to use this gift we receive tonight. I want each of you to pick one thing you can work on, just one thing you can change for the better, right here in our community."

Murmurs rippled through the congregation.

"I want you to give this idea some serious thought," Pastor Daniels said. "But don't take too long. When Reverend Dr. King visited with us here in Detroit last summer, he said, '*Now* is the time to lift our nation.' Now is the time, New Hope, for us to lift *our* nation. Now is the time for you"—he pointed one way—"and you"—he pointed the other way—"and you! To take action!"

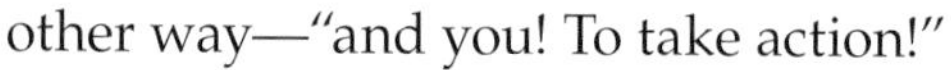

Melody was sure he was looking directly at her. She held her breath.

"The new year, 1964, is a season of change. Change yourself. Change our community. Change our nation!"

Miss Dorothy, who directed Melody and her friends in the children's choir, began to play the piano. The adult choir rose and began to sing. Melody sang along, clapping in time with the rhythm.

We've come this far by faith,
Leaning on the Lord,
Trusting in His holy word,
He's never failed me yet.
Oh, oh, oh, can't turn around,
We've come this far by faith.

As the song ended, the church bells sounded, drowning out the final piano notes. It was midnight! It was 1964!

"Happy New Year!" Pastor Daniels shouted.

"Happy birthday, Melody!" Val shouted, too, squeezing Melody in a hug. But in the din of bells and cheers and applause, only Melody heard her.

♫

The Watch Night celebration continued downstairs in the church hall, where everyone greeted each other saying "Happy New Year!" Melody, Val, and Lila stood in line with Yvonne to get cookies, while the rest of the family found seats at one of the tables. Yvonne chatted about Pastor Daniels's sermon with the man in front of her. Melody tried to spot her best friend, Sharon, in the crowd, but the room was packed.

"There's Diane," Val said.

Melody saw her friend Diane Harris helping her little sisters carry cups of punch. Across the hall Melody saw

Miss Esther Collins sitting with a group of other elderly people. Miss Esther was a neighbor who loved gardening just as much as Melody did. She looked up and waved. Melody smiled and waved back.

Val nudged Melody when the lady behind them commented on how pretty the amaryllis flowers were. Melody smiled and tried not to yawn. She didn't want anyone to think she was still too young to be at Watch Night.

With cookies stacked on napkins, Yvonne led them back to the table where the rest of their family was sitting. Melody took the chair next to her grandmother. Everyone in Melody's family called her grandmother Big Momma, even though she was barely taller than Melody. The name was a sign of respect.

Big Momma put her arm around Melody. "You did a beautiful job with the decorations, chick." Big Momma called her grandchildren chicks.

"*Everyone* is talking about them," Val said, passing around the cookies.

"And Pastor Daniels's Challenge to Change," Yvonne added. "I'm going to take the challenge with me when I go back to school. I'm not sure what I'll do on campus, but I know what I can do in another community. There's talk about students going to Mississippi this summer for a civil rights project. I want to go."

Melody's mother shifted in her seat. "What exactly would you all be doing?" she asked.

"A bunch of things. I heard there will be more voter registration, and volunteers will talk to black folks to remind them that they have a say in how this country works. I think they'll also be setting up community centers and schools. I might try working with kids." Yvonne was speaking fast, the way she did when she was excited about an idea.

"Teaching?" Melody asked. "Just like Mommy!" Melody looked at their mother, who looked pleased.

"I thought you were studying business," pointed out Lila, who liked to get all the facts straight.

Yvonne laughed. "I am, Lila. But let's just say that I want to make it my business to help teach black history. Schools are really poor in the South. Lots of kids in black communities don't know about the contributions black Americans have made."

"You mean like Dr. King?" Melody asked.

"And many others," Big Momma said. "Harriet Tubman, Frederick Douglass, and Mrs. Rosa Parks."

"Yes, yes!" Yvonne was bouncing in her seat. "I think when you know about your history, and when you're proud of it, it makes you stronger."

"We're proud of you," Melody's father said, looking

steadily at Yvonne. "However." Daddy paused to lean forward so that his arms rested on the table. "I want you to be careful in Mississippi and to be safe."

Yvonne laughed. "I know, Dad." But when Daddy gave her a stern look, Yvonne said, "Yes, sir."

"What about you chicks?" Big Momma said to Melody and Val. "What are you going to do with your gift?"

"Us?" Val replied. "Did Pastor Daniels mean kids, too?"

"Of course he meant kids, too," Melody said excitedly.

"He certainly did," Big Momma said as the grown-ups around the table nodded and smiled.

Suddenly, Yvonne slipped her arm around Melody's shoulder. "Speaking of gifts, somebody should be thinking about her birthday gifts."

"That's right!" Lila slapped the table with her hand. "Dee-Dee is officially ten years old!"

"I am," Melody said, realizing that she'd just stayed awake past midnight for the first time ever. The new year had begun, and it was her birthday. As she blinked away sleep, she thought about Pastor Daniels's challenge and wondered what great big idea would come her way.

Double-Digits Birthday

CHAPTER 3

In the afternoon on New Year's Day, Melody sorted through the neat stack of records in the living room to find just the right music for her birthday celebration. As she flipped past names she'd heard on the radio or seen on TV, she imagined one day picking up a record with Dwayne's name on it.

Melody was only halfway through the stack when the doorbell rang.

"*Happy birthday to yooouuu!*" Sharon and Diane sang as Melody opened the door. Diane gave Melody a tube-shaped package tied with yarn at either end. It looked like a big piece of candy.

Sharon handed Melody a soft, tissue-paper-wrapped package. "Sorry, it got a little squished," she said.

"Thanks," Melody said. She put the packages on the coffee table and motioned toward the record player. "I'm trying to find some music."

"Wouldn't it be great if your brother and his group could be here to sing?" Sharon asked.

"Yeah! A live concert would be so cool!" Diane said.

"It would," Melody nodded, thinking about how much she missed her brother. "But The Three Ravens aren't in Detroit. They sang at a New Year's Eve concert somewhere in Ohio last night."

"Too bad," Sharon said, sorting through the records lying on the sofa. "Hey! Here's Little Stevie Wonder's 'Fingertips.'" Melody put the record on the turntable and carefully moved the needle arm to its edge.

"*This* is birthday music!" Sharon hopped up, and the girls began to dance. They danced their way across the floor and into the dining room.

Melody barely dodged the kitchen door as her mother opened it, carrying a triple-chocolate cake on a blue glass plate.

"Whoa, there, birthday girl!" Mommy said, placing the cake safely in the center of the table. Melody stopped. Sharon and Diane froze.

"Sorry, Mommy!" Melody said, still bopping her head to the music.

Melody's mother smiled and shook her shoulders and bopped her head a few beats, too. Sharon burst out laughing.

Mommy shrugged. "Who can keep still when it's Little Stevie Wonder?" she asked.

As if the music had stirred the entire house into movement, all at once Daddy, Yvonne, and Lila trooped downstairs. Then there was a knock at the front door, and at the same time the telephone rang and someone was coming into the kitchen from the back door.

Mommy went into the kitchen to answer the phone as Yvonne answered the front door. In came Melody's grandparents and her cousins. In the blink of an eye, the dining room was filled with people and noise. Melody didn't know which way to turn.

"Happy birthday, chick!" Big Momma was first to give Melody a hug.

"Big ten!" Cousin Charles said. "Congratulations!"

"Happy birthday, baby." Cousin Tish gave Melody a kiss. "Love that hairstyle," she whispered, fluffing Melody's curled bangs.

Val hugged Melody and handed her a small box with a bow on it. "This is for you," Val said. "Happy, happy!"

"How about we get some candles for this cake and celebrate our birthday girl?" Melody's father called above the noise.

"Here we go!" Yvonne placed ten tiny blue candles in a circle atop the chocolate frosting, and then stuck another one in the middle.

"To grow on," she laughed.

"Ready to sing, everybody?" Lila turned off the record player and pulled Melody to stand right in front of her cake, while Daddy lit the candles.

"Where's Mommy?" Melody looked over her shoulder.

"Here!" Her mother stepped in from the kitchen, breathless.

"Happy birthday to you. Happy birthday to you. Happy birthday, dear Melody. Happy birthday to you!"

Melody was beaming. She loved when her family sang together—it was almost like they had their own choir, the way all their voices blended and harmonized in just the right ways! She took a breath but didn't blow out the candles yet. In her family, there was one more verse of the birthday song to sing. Melody smiled and looked around at all their faces, waiting. Suddenly, a solo voice came from the kitchen. It was a high tenor, almost like Smokey Robinson's.

"How o-old are you? How o-old are you? My kid sister, Dee-Dee . . ."

"Dwayne!" Melody squealed, throwing open the kitchen door.

"How o-old are you?" Dwayne finished singing and gave her a bear hug. "Didn't I tell you when I left that I'd show up when you didn't expect it? Happy birthday!"

Melody pulled Dwayne into the room.

"Well, I declare!" Tish laughed.

"When did you get here?" Lila asked.

Melody noticed that the only people who didn't seem surprised were her mother and father.

"Parents know how to keep secrets, too," Daddy said. "And it was a good one, wasn't it?"

"The best ever!" Melody agreed. Since Dwayne had started working for Motown, he was rarely at home. And when his singing group did come back to town, he spent more time at the studio and at his bandmate Phil's house than he did with the family. Their father wasn't very happy about that, but now Daddy and Dwayne were both smiling, and Melody was glad her birthday had brought them together.

"Blow out the candles, and let's cut this cake," Dwayne said. "I'm starved!" He turned to Melody and gave her a bow. "Birthday girls first, of course."

Melody sat on the floor between Diane and Val with her paper party plate balanced on her knees. Everyone was listening to her brother's stories about traveling around the country with the famous Motown singers. He was telling how he'd accidentally almost tripped one of The Supremes backstage when Val nudged Melody with an elbow.

"When are you going to open your presents?" she whispered, not very quietly.

Dwayne stopped midsentence. "Oh, yeah. Mine first." Dwayne went back into the kitchen and came out carrying a record album. "I didn't exactly have time to wrap it," he told his sister.

Melody looked carefully at the bright red cover and the three young black women looking over their shoulders in the picture. Big orange letters announced the album's artists, Martha and The Vandellas. The album was called *Heat Wave*. That was the name of one of Melody's favorite songs.

Scrawled across the lower corner was a handwritten message. Melody read it out loud: *"Happy birthday, Dee-Dee. Stay cool. Martha."* Melody's mouth dropped open.

Sharon, Val, and Lila crowded around to see.

"Wow, Dwayne! Martha Reeves is one of the hottest stars at Motown right now," Yvonne said. "She's world famous!"

Melody looked at Dwayne. "You got Martha Reeves to autograph it for *me*?" she asked.

Dwayne shrugged and nodded, but he looked pleased that Melody liked her gift.

"Do you really know her?" Sharon asked, starstruck.

"Sort of," he said. "I mean, we're at the studio at the same time . . . sometimes."

"Thank you, Dwayne," Melody said. "You're the best brother ever."

"That's something special," Big Momma said. As Melody passed the album to her grandmother, she saw her father squinting at it.

"How long before we see your face on something like this?" Daddy asked, looking over at Dwayne. Melody shot a look at her brother.

"Dad, I know I have a long way to go. I'm working real hard at it. I'm hoping to get into the studio to record my own music soon."

"I know you'll be as famous as Martha Reeves one day," Melody said confidently. But Daddy just shook his head.

Dwayne turned the record player on and snapped his fingers when music began to play. "Isn't this a dancing party?" He reached for Melody's hand and pulled her up from the floor. "Come on, Dee-Dee Double Digits. Let's dance!"

Melody followed Dwayne's smooth steps toward the dining room, where the floor was clear. In seconds, Charles had gotten Tish up, Lila and Yvonne were moving to the beat, and Val and Sharon were doing a silly bird-like step.

"Are you back to stay? Did you write any new songs? When are you going to make your own record?" Melody asked Dwayne all at once.

"So many questions!" he laughed. "Am I on a quiz show?"

"No," Melody answered. "I missed you, that's all."

"In that case, we're in town for a while to sing backup for some folks and work on a new song I wrote."

"How does it go?"

Dwayne sang loud enough for Melody to hear over the record that was playing:

Girl, it's time that I move,
Time for movin' on up.
Yeah, it's time for my move,
Time to start changing my luck.

"Oh, that sounds good," Melody said. "I like it."

"I do, too," Dwayne told her. "When we get studio time, I want you to sing it with me. I'm not kidding!"

"I know you're not," Melody smiled. But right now she couldn't imagine anything better than this wonderful moment.

Dwayne took her by one hand and spun her around. She almost felt as if she were flying. Everyone was laughing. Her grandparents were clapping. She looked over her shoulder and saw her mother and father dancing, too. She closed her eyes to take a picture with her mind. She felt happy. She felt strong, as if she could do anything.

The Block Club

♫ CHAPTER 4 ♫

The following Friday evening, Melody and Lila helped their mother tidy up. The Ellisons were hosting a meeting of the Block Club. Once a month, several families from the neighborhood got together, and the kids played games while their parents talked about what was going on in Detroit and in their community.

Dwayne brought up folding chairs from the basement. Then he stood brushing dust off his pants.

Melody stopped stacking Daddy's newspapers for a moment and looked at her brother, remembering last summer, when he had worked at the auto factory after graduating from high school. He'd come home from his shift dirty then, too. Now he was almost always neat and clean and had a fresh haircut. She giggled.

"What?" Dwayne smiled.

"Nothing. It's just so great that you're at home for a while," she said.

"Home?" Lila shook her dusting rag in Dwayne's direction. "He's never at home. He's always over at Motown, acting like singing is real work."

"It is real work! We don't just sing. We have classes on how to dress, how to talk if we get interviewed by reporters, even how to eat in a fancy restaurant. And . . ." Dwayne spun in one of the new moves that he'd learned. "We get dance lessons from a real choreographer."

Mommy was nodding her approval. "Mr. Berry Gordy must care a lot about how his performers behave," she said.

"Yes, he does," Dwayne said.

Lila shrugged and kept dusting.

Dwayne snapped his fingers in her direction. "If you feel like that, Lila, I guess you don't want an invite to see Hitsville U.S.A. up close and get a tour of the Motown studio, huh?"

Lila froze. "Wh-what?"

"I do! I do!" Melody shouted.

"So do I," Mommy said.

"I'll see what I can do," Dwayne answered. Melody thought he sounded very important.

Dwayne looked at his watch. "Speaking of the studio, I gotta run. The Three Ravens are doing backup for a new singer. Bye!"

Melody's mother had a funny look on her face as Dwayne pecked her on the cheek and rushed away. After he left, Mommy shook her head. "I do wish Dwayne were going to college," she said, almost to herself. "Still, he's turning into quite a young man."

"Does Daddy think so?" Lila asked.

Melody was wondering the same thing.

"Your father is proud of all of you," Mommy said firmly. "Let's get the sandwiches made. People will start showing up in less than an hour!"

They were all heading to the kitchen when the doorbell rang. "I'll get it," Melody said, wondering who was arriving so early.

"Miss Esther!" Melody said when she opened the door. "Come in."

"I know I'm early for the meeting," Miss Esther said, tapping her way into the living room with her cane. "But I have something for you."

"Please sit down," Melody said, using her best company manners. Even though Miss Esther was more like family than company.

"I'm so sorry I missed your birthday celebration," Miss Esther said. "So tonight I came before the others to give you a belated gift." She opened her purse and took out a small burlap pouch that was no larger than Melody's hands.

"Thank you," Melody said, sitting down on the sofa.

She peeked inside the pouch. "Seeds!" She smiled at Miss Esther. "What kind are they?"

"Those are hollyhocks, and they're very special. They're called 'heirlooms.' They grow from seeds that are collected from plants every year and passed on from generation to generation."

Melody's face lit up. Poppa had taught her about heirloom plants. He'd taken her many times to the botanical gardens at Belle Isle Park. He said some of the plants came from seeds that were one hundred years old. "My grandfather calls heirloom plants 'great-great-grandflowers,'" Melody said.

"Is that right?" Miss Esther laughed.

"Oh, I can't wait to plant these," Melody said.

"They'll grow almost as tall as you are," Miss Esther said. "I brought them up from my mother's garden in Alabama when I first came to Detroit as a young woman. I had a big, beautiful garden at my first home here in the city. Now I don't have the space—or the energy—for one."

Melody wanted to ask lots of questions, like where in Alabama Miss Esther came from, and what kind of garden she had, and what her other Detroit house had looked like. But before she could say anything, Miss Esther put her hand on Melody's arm.

"I knew I'd picked the right young person to hand

these heirlooms down to. We can talk more about how and where to plant them another time, all right?"

"Yes, ma'am," Melody said. Miss Esther's confidence in her made Melody feel special.

Right then Melody's mother came out of the kitchen holding a plate piled with triangle-shaped sandwiches. "Hello, Miss Esther! How are you this evening?"

"I am well, thank you, Frances," Miss Esther said. "Melody and I have been discussing gardening."

While her mother and Miss Esther chatted, Melody went upstairs to put the burlap pouch away in her dresser drawer and grab her pack of Old Maid playing cards. When she went back downstairs, the living room was crowded with familiar faces. There was Sharon's mother, and Diane's parents, and the parents of Julius Sterling, a boy from school. In the kitchen, Julius, Val, Sharon, and Diane were sitting at the table, munching on popcorn.

"Hi, everybody," Melody said.

"This meeting is going to be boring," Diane said, folding her arms across her chest.

"It doesn't have to be," Melody said. "I brought my Old Maid cards."

Sharon waved her bingo game in the air, but Julius plunked a box on the table.

"Dominoes." He looked around at all the girls.

"Anybody know how to play?"

"I do," Melody and Sharon said at the same time.

"Me, too," Val said, nodding. "My daddy showed me."

Diane unfolded her arms and relaxed. "I do, too. My granddad taught me," she said. "I'll play!"

Melody sat down. Two games and one big bowl of popcorn later, everyone was having a good time. As Diane was adding up the score, the adult voices in the other room got louder. The kids stopped their own conversation to listen. Melody got up from her chair and went to ease the door open a crack.

"I tell you, we need to do something about the new management at Fieldston's Clothing Store," someone said. "They're right here in a Negro community, but they act as if every Negro customer is there to steal something!"

Melody thought about what had happened to her and Dwayne when they had been shopping at Fieldston's last spring. Without thinking, she opened the door wide and barged into the living room.

"Fieldston's *does* discriminate against black people!" she said, walking into the middle of the circle of chairs.

All eyes turned toward Melody, including her parents' and Miss Esther's.

"And how do you know that?" Diane's mother asked, surprised.

"I know because the manager accused *me* of shoplifting," she said.

"Say what?" Her father half rose from his chair. Mommy put a hand on his arm.

"When was this?" Mommy asked.

"It was last spring. I went to help Dwayne pick out a suit," Melody said. The memory made her angry. "Dwayne was just trying on a jacket, and the manager made him take it off. Then he started yelling and made us leave the store before we could buy anything. I don't think we should spend our money in a store that treats us like that."

"That's not right," Melody's father said. "Old Mr. Fieldston never would have stood for that when he was alive."

Julius's father was nodding. "My butcher shop is just a few doors up from Fieldston's, and I hear the same story over and over. I think we ought to protest by boycotting Fieldston's."

"You mean not shop there at all?" Mrs. Harris said.

"Yes," Melody's father answered. "And I say we picket in front of the store, too. We can hand out leaflets that explain how they treat black customers. They may not want to notice us, but they notice our money. And they'll notice when it's gone."

Melody's stomach felt trembly as she thought of the TV

news reports of black and white people protesting against racial discrimination. Sometimes there were police, and the protesters got arrested.

"You're talking about carrying signs?" Charles asked.

Miss Esther cleared her throat. "I don't see why not. We should speak up with our voices," she said, giving Melody an approving look. "And with our pocketbooks."

Miss Esther's comment made Melody realize that some of the other adults thought she should be quiet. But she couldn't. She turned to her mother. "You told me that what we do with our money says a lot about what we believe."

"I did say that," her mother said. "Thank you for reminding me, Melody. I think we should consider Miss Esther's and Mr. Sterling's suggestions." She glanced around the room. "Melody, I think that concludes your part of the meeting," she said gently.

There was a buzz of reaction as Melody left the room. The kitchen door was wide open, and her friends were bunched in the doorway, staring at her.

"Oh, my goodness!" Val dragged Melody into the kitchen. "I can't believe you went out there and interrupted the meeting."

Melody thought of Yvonne, who always told her to use her voice and speak up about fairness. She knew Yvonne would be pleased.

"Do you really think people will boycott Fieldston's?" Diane asked. "My mom shops there all the time."

"She won't be able to if there's a picket line in front of the store," Julius said.

"I saw picket lines in Birmingham," Val said. "People carried signs and marched in front of restaurants and stores that wouldn't serve black people."

All of a sudden, Melody made a decision. "I'm going to make a picket sign, and I'm going to carry it in the protest. If my parents let me."

"Are you nuts?" Julius asked.

Melody just shook her head. "This is about being fair. Maybe a boycott will make Fieldston's change. Wouldn't that be better for everybody?"

"Mostly for our parents," Julius said.

"That's not true," Val said. "If our parents don't get treated fairly, we don't either. In Alabama a sign on a water fountain that says 'Whites Only' means grown-ups *and* kids. That's why kids have been standing up and marching for equal rights."

Diane nodded. "Maybe all of us kids should march."

"Yes," Melody said. "And maybe there are other things we could do around here to prove that kids can make things better, too."

We March!

CHAPTER 5

On the first Saturday in February, a group gathered in front of Julius's father's butcher shop. Even though it was cold, almost fifty people had shown up to protest. Melody stood in a line with her mother while her father walked among the people, passing out leaflets and some of the signs that had been piling up at the Ellisons' house. Melody had made her own sign. It said, "Support Our Boycott!" She was ready to hold it up high and march.

The picketing was to begin at ten thirty, and by then the line was even longer. Melody saw Diane and her parents, and Sharon with her mother. She saw kids from school and one or two teachers. Lila was up ahead, standing with her friends. Julius's father appeared at the door of his shop, took off his apron, and handed it to someone inside. Then he took Julius by the hand and stepped to the front of the line. He bent to pick up a sign.

"Shop in Dignity!" he chanted, walking slowly along the sidewalk.

Melody got a good grip on her sign and began to pick up the chant. At the corner past Fieldston's, the line crossed the street and marched on the other side. People turned their signs so that anyone looking out of the Fieldston's window could read them.

Many of the protesters looked straight ahead when they walked past the Fieldston's display window, but Melody couldn't. When she was in front of the store, she turned to stare. She found herself looking right at the same man—the manager—who'd yelled at her and Dwayne. For a second their eyes locked.

Do you recognize me? Melody wondered. Maybe he had falsely accused so many people that he didn't remember her. Other clerks joined the manager at the display window. Some looked shocked. One woman looked angry. But they all stood frozen, almost like mannequins.

Melody kept her eyes on the window after she passed the store. She saw a white man stop at the door. But Melody's father handed the man one of the leaflets. The man read it, and then backed away and left without crossing the picket line.

Someone began to sing. Melody didn't recognize the voice, but she knew the song. She sang along.

We shall not,
We shall not be moved.

The chanting stopped and the singing grew louder.

We shall not,
We shall not be moved.
Just like a tree that's standing by the water,
We shall not be moved.

But then the words changed. Melody hummed along, listening to the part she'd never heard before.

We're fighting for our children,
We shall not be moved.

Melody was at the corner. She looked at the line and

guessed there were now at least one hundred people protesting. She saw a young man, wearing a hat pulled low, ease between two of the marchers.

It was Dwayne!

Melody was surprised. Last year, Dwayne had refused to go with the family to the Walk to Freedom, even though it had been a huge event and Dr. King had given a speech. Dwayne had said that he didn't think marches could change anything and that becoming a rich and famous singer was what would make people treat him fairly. But Melody knew, from the letters he'd sent home while he was touring, that Dwayne had changed his mind. He had told her that even the Motown stars were treated unfairly at some hotels and restaurants. *Seems like our talent is colored first, and great second,* he had written.

Now her brother spotted her. Their eyes met and held for a moment. Then Dwayne shook his head. Melody understood that he didn't want her to tell anyone he was there. Melody pinched her thumb and finger together and slid them across her lips as if she were closing a zipper. It was their "I won't tell" signal.

Dwayne tugged his hat lower, and Melody crossed the street. When she looked, Dwayne's part of the line had passed the window at Fieldston's, and he was gone.

Melody kept walking and singing. She sang as loud as

she could, becoming part of the rhythm of voices. Melody realized that because of her own experience at Fieldston's, she was connected to people she would never know: the people from the past who had been treated unfairly, just as she and Dwayne had been, and people in the future. After all, if their boycott was a success, Fieldston's would change.

Melody was part of that change.

It was late afternoon when Melody and her family returned home from picketing. Big Momma was there with a casserole for their supper, and Val was with her. "The boycott made the news on the radio," Val said. "I wish I'd been there."

"Maybe your parents will let you come next week," Melody said as she took off her coat. Charles and Tish supported equal rights, but Val's father had said that in Alabama, being part of even a peaceful march or protest could cause a black man to lose his job—or get put in jail. "There wasn't any trouble today," Melody added. "There weren't even any police there."

Melody sat down on the sofa and wrapped a blanket around her shoulders. She was cold. Her legs were tired from walking, and her arms were tired from holding up her protest sign. But her heart felt stronger because she had been part of something she believed in.

Wish List

CHAPTER 6

The next day, after church and dinner at Big Momma's, Melody took Bo for a walk. Her brain was busy thinking about how the Fieldston's protest had gone. Everyone at New Hope had been talking about it, and Pastor Daniels even mentioned it in his sermon.

Now Bo stopped across the street from Miss Esther's bright yellow house to sniff at something underneath the snow. That's when Melody realized that they were standing outside the community playground. She hadn't played there in ages! Along the chain-link fence, Melody looked for the sign that read "Park closes at dusk." But she couldn't find it—a wild tangle of a hedge had grown up almost as tall as the fence. Melody frowned at how messy it looked.

The gate was open, so Melody and Bo went in. It was a Sunday afternoon and not very cold, but the playground was empty. Melody looked around. There had once been flower beds along the fence, but Melody couldn't remember seeing anything blooming in the park last summer. Now all she could see were clumps of dead weeds and uncut grass bunched in the snow.

She smiled, remembering how Yvonne had helped her climb the jungle gym when she was little. But now the bars were rusting. Melody turned to the swings, remembering Dwayne pushing her and Lila and singing a made-up song:

Dee-Dee and Lila flying so high,
Two little sisters touching the sky!

Now, three of the four swings were missing, and the remaining one was dangling from a broken chain, the seat touching the ground. Some of the bricks were missing from the handball courts, and others were crumbling. The paint on the benches was peeling, and the dented trash can was tipped over. It didn't look like anyone was paying attention to the park.

Melody shook her head. No wonder no one was using it. "This used to be such a fun place to play," she said to Bo. "Somebody should do something."

Bo looked up at her and barked.

"Me?" Melody bent to tickle the spot between Bo's ears. "I don't know . . ." She took another slow walk around the paths, and as she did her brain got busy again. But this time, she was imagining the playground filled with kids having fun. She pictured a shiny new jungle gym, spiffy swings, and tons of beautiful flowers. There could be a vegetable garden, and even a stage for music shows.

Melody felt her heart pounding with excitement. Fixing up the playground could be her own special way of making things better in her community. "This is it, Bo!" Melody said. "This is *my* Challenge to Change."

Melody tugged Bo's leash. "Come on," she said. Her big sister was just the person to help her figure out where to begin. She wanted to write Yvonne a letter right away. Melody started to run.

♫

On Saturday, Melody got a letter from Yvonne.

Dear Dee-Dee,

I'm so proud of you for wanting to clean up the park. I loved going there and playing on the jungle gym with you and Lila when you were little. Remember how you loved to go down the slide but were afraid to climb up the ladder? I helped you up the steps, and we sailed down the slide together.

I think it's a great answer to the Challenge to Change.

It's a big job, but I bet the other kids in the neighborhood will work with you. It would be fun to do it together. Just ask them. Oh, and don't be afraid to ask for help from a grown-up. Remember what Pastor Daniels said: It's a season of change!

Let me know how things go.

Love, Vonnie

Melody folded the letter. She knew her sister was right about asking for help. And tomorrow, Melody would do just that.

After church service, Melody and Val headed downstairs to Sunday school. Melody was eager to talk to her friends about her answer to the Challenge to Change. "Hi, everybody," she said, stopping them at the classroom door. "I have an idea, but I need help."

Sharon leaned in. "What kind of help?"

"What's the idea?" Diane asked.

"The last time you had an idea," Julius said, "you ended up talking in front of the whole Block Club."

Melody took a deep breath and let the words tumble out. "The playground in our neighborhood is a mess, and I want to make it nice again!"

"I didn't know there was a playground," Val said.

Julius nodded. "My dad taught me how to play handball there."

"Nobody goes there anymore," Sharon said. "Maybe we're just too old for jungle gyms!"

"Well, my little sisters aren't," Diane said. "I took them there last summer, and most of the swings were gone. The one that's left is broken. My mom says it's dangerous."

"I think having a fun, safe playground is really important," Melody said. Most people in their neighborhood had small backyards. A few had swing sets, but many had vegetable gardens instead, like her family did. "If we work together as a team, maybe we could fix it up," she continued. "We could clean it up, paint the benches, pull out the weeds, and plant flowers—"

"Get new swings," Diane added.

"And maybe do something about the handball courts," Julius said hopefully.

Melody was encouraged. Her friends were getting excited. So she told them the rest of her idea. "What if we start our own club, a kids' block club?"

There was silence for a moment. Then Julius nodded. "Count me in."

"Great idea!" Sharon said.

Diane smiled and nodded her agreement.

"I'll join for now," Val said "but don't you think we

might have to ask permission or something—President Melody?"

"P . . . Pres . . ." Melody stuttered and blinked. *President?* She'd never intended to be a leader, just part of the club. It would be like the choir here at church, where she was one voice among many. Being the president of something meant being a leader—like Miss Dorothy or Pastor Daniels. Melody wasn't so sure she could do that.

"Don't try to get out of it now," Julius laughed. "It was your idea."

"I . . . um . . . okay," Melody stammered. "Let's start by asking the grown-ups' Block Club."

Sunday school began, but Melody's mind was still on the playground. Her friends were excited, but they wanted her to lead. That seemed like a job for a grown-up.

Wait. Hadn't Yvonne told Melody not to be afraid to ask for help from a grown-up? Suddenly, Melody knew just the right person.

♫

That afternoon, Melody went to Miss Esther's house. After she rang the bell, Melody turned around to look at Miss Esther's view of the park. It wasn't pretty.

When Miss Esther opened the door, she was happy to see Melody. "What a nice surprise!" she said. "Come in, come in." Miss Esther went to sit in a soft armchair near the front window. She gestured toward another chair, and Melody sat, too.

"Do you always sit at this window?" Melody asked.

"I like to see what's going on in the neighborhood."

"Do you like what you see? Over at the park, I mean."

Miss Esther sighed. "I can't say that I do like it, Melody. It's in such bad shape." She leaned forward. "Why do you ask?"

"Well, I sort of have a plan for it."

"I'm so glad to hear it!" Miss Esther said.

Melody scooted to the edge of her chair. "I want to answer the New Year's Challenge to Change by cleaning up the playground and planting a garden. I talked to some of my friends, and they want to help, too. We want to start a Junior Block Club."

"If you take your idea to the Block Club, you'll need a plan in writing to explain what you hope to do," Miss Esther said.

"Oh," Melody said, sitting back in her chair. "I don't know how to do that." Suddenly she felt discouraged.

"Well," Miss Esther said, getting up from her chair, "perhaps I can help. Let's start by making a list of everything you'd like to do. I call that the 'wish list,' because sometimes the plan changes and you don't get to do everything you wish you could do."

And with that, Melody and Miss Esther began to work together.

On the first Friday in March, Melody and her parents walked to Julius's house after dinner for the monthly Block Club meeting. Everyone gathered in the finished basement, where the grown-ups sat on folding chairs around card tables and drank coffee out of paper cups. Melody, Val, Sharon, Diane, and Julius perched on some stools.

At seven o'clock, Mr. Sterling quieted the group and began the meeting.

"Welcome, folks! I want to start with a quick update about the progress of the Fieldston's boycott. We've had some newspaper coverage, and one of the TV stations is interested in doing a story. So we have to keep up the pressure and keep up our protests. We all know that change doesn't happen overnight."

There was applause from the kids and the grown-ups. When the group was quiet again, Mr. Sterling said, "Now, some of the children want to speak."

Melody took a piece of paper out of her pocket. It was the wish list Miss Esther had helped her write. "Hello," she said, looking around the room. Her father raised his chin and smiled. She saw Miss Esther on the far side of the large room.

"We—all of us up here—would like to ask permission to start a Junior Block Club. The reason, um, our purpose, is to fix up the playground and change that part of our community for everyone."

"What a good idea," Sharon's father said from his seat. "It's a disgrace how the city has let that playground deteriorate." Other parents murmured in agreement.

Diane's mother raised her hand. Melody felt funny giving a grown-up permission to speak. "Yes?" Melody said in her best leader voice.

"Do you children have a plan?" Mrs. Harris asked.

"Yes, ma'am, we do," Melody said. As she read her wish list aloud, there were nods of approval.

Miss Esther tapped her cane on the linoleum floor. "I move that we allow the formation of a Junior Block Club."

Melody's father raised his hand. "I second that motion."

"Good! Let's vote!" Mr. Sterling said. "Raise hands to vote yes for a Junior Block Club."

Melody was holding her breath. Every hand went up.

"The ayes have it! Congratulations, Junior Block Club," Mr. Sterling announced.

Melody turned to her friends. They all jumped off their stools and cheered. Julius started shaking the girls' hands.

Mr. Sterling cleared his throat. "Now, you *do* need an adult adviser."

"I have already been asked to assist, and I've accepted the position," Miss Esther said with another tap of her cane.

"And Melody is our president!" Julius shouted. The adults laughed and clapped again.

Melody's father spoke up. "Well, Junior Block Club, do you think you can have this playground cleaned up and ready for our annual Block Club picnic?"

"The picnic is August first, right?" Julius asked.

"Yes," his father said.

"That's almost five months away," Sharon said, counting on her fingers. "That's a lot of time."

Melody didn't say anything. She knew that growing a garden could take a long time. But her friends were so excited, and they were all eager to help, so Melody nodded her head. "We'll make it work," she said.

Grandfathers and "Grand-Flowers"

CHAPTER 7

Melody and Val were in Big Momma's kitchen helping get Sunday dinner ready. On the ride from church, the girls had told Melody's grandparents all about the Junior Block Club and their plans for the park. Poppa and Big Momma were excited about the way Melody and Val and their friends were answering the Challenge to Change, and they had offered to help.

"Oh, good," Melody had said as the car pulled into the driveway. "Because we don't know how to do some of the stuff we want to."

Big Momma's kitchen smelled of baked chicken and homemade rolls. She put Val to work opening a jar of green beans that she and Melody's mother had canned last summer. Val poured the green beans into a pan for Big Momma to heat.

As Melody set the table, the rest of the family trickled in. When Dwayne arrived, he said, "What's this I hear about Melody becoming president of the Junior Block Club?"

"How did you find out?" Melody asked, setting the salt

and pepper shakers in the center of the table.

"I have my neighborhood connections," Dwayne said, winking.

After Poppa said grace and they began to pass the food around, Melody and Val took turns explaining the park project. When they got to the list of things they didn't know how to fix, Melody frowned. "The handball courts are falling apart," she said. "They're made of brick. What should we do?"

"The father of one of my piano students is a bricklayer," Big Momma said. "I could talk to him."

"Would you, Big Momma?" Melody asked eagerly. "And Poppa, would you help us decide which plants would grow best in the park?"

"I will," he said, passing the bowl of beans to Charles. "You'll need to draw up a plan of the space so we know how much room we have."

"What about the swings?" Val asked. "We want to get ones that aren't broken."

"I think that replacing the swings is the city's responsibility," Mommy replied. "You can ask the Parks Commissioner. How do you think you can find his name?" she asked in her teacher's voice.

Melody and Val looked at each other and shrugged.

Lila rolled her eyes. "The library," she sighed.

Charles took a serving of green beans and looked across the table at Melody's mother. "Frances, this reminds me of all the canning you and Big Momma did when we were kids.

Big Momma laughed. "It was quite a lot of work every summer to can all those fruits and vegetables."

"But they tasted so good," Charles said.

"What did you grow, Poppa?" Melody asked.

"A little bit of everything," Poppa answered. "I had pecan trees and peanuts. Greens of all kinds, beans, tomatoes, potatoes."

"That sounds like a grocery store," Dwayne laughed.

"Yes, it pretty much was," Big Momma said. "In those days, we grew everything we ate. We planted, we weeded, we picked. If we had an extra-large crop of something, we'd share with neighbors."

"I loved that place," Poppa said, his voice becoming thicker and quieter. "See, I'd grown up on that farm. My daddy worked it for a white man. He worked hard. We worked hard with him." Poppa looked down at his knife and fork for a few moments, and then looked up again. Everyone had stopped eating to listen. "I knew how much my daddy wanted to own that place, so I worked extra jobs to help. Daddy scrimped and saved. Together, we finally saved enough to be able to buy a little piece of that land."

He looked toward Big Momma, who smiled and put her hand over his on the table.

"Back then it was almost impossible for a Negro to own property," she said. "Not long after they bought the land, Frank's father died. So Frank took over the farm. We had only just gotten married. His sister Beck and his brother Roy—that's Charles's daddy—had already left and moved to Birmingham. I was teaching music at a school during the week and giving piano lessons on the weekends. Your grandfather worked hard day and night to keep the farm going."

"That land was special to me," Poppa said. "It was more than just dirt and trees and plants. It was . . . my life. It had been my daddy's life and my mama's life. Hardest thing I ever did was leave it. But . . ."

He looked around at Val and Melody and Lila and Dwayne. "I did it for all of you. I passed it on to all of you."

Lila shook her head. "How could you pass it on, Poppa? We've never even seen it."

"You have it in you," Poppa said to Lila. "It's the way your parents teach you and how you work hard." He turned to Dwayne. "It's what we share, like our love of music." Finally, Poppa looked at Melody. "It's me teaching you about plants. How to make them grow tall and strong. How to make things beautiful. And you know what? One day you'll pass my farm on to the children you have."

Poppa tapped his chest. "It's here."

Everyone at the table was quiet. Melody saw Tish dabbing at her eyes with her paper napkin. Big Momma still had her hand over Poppa's. Mommy looked as if she was remembering something from long ago.

"You know what, Poppa?" Dwayne said. "I know what you mean. It was hard for me to leave home, too." For once, Dwayne was very serious. "I miss all of this, sitting around talking and eating Mom's and Big Momma's great food together." He looked at his father. "I even miss you yelling at me about college."

Daddy started to say something, but Dwayne went on.

"But like Poppa said, all of you are here." He tapped his chest. "So every time I write a song, or sing a song, I've got all the Ellisons and Porters right with me. Dad, I know you think I got into this business for all the wrong reasons, for flash and fame. You were kind of right. It's hard work. I know that you and your father, and Poppa and his daddy—y'all broke your backs working hard to give us an easier life than you had. It's not easy being black, no matter what we choose to do, right? I still believe that music can change things, and I'm not afraid to work hard at something I want. I learned that from you, Dad."

Melody's father looked confused and proud all at once.

He stared at Dwayne, but neither one of them said a word.

Melody finally broke the silence. "I'd like to see the farm," she said.

Her grandfather smiled. "And you will, Little One. I'll make sure of it." He turned toward Melody's mother. "Let's drive down once school is out, Frances. I'll get someone to take care of the shop for a week, and we can stay with my sister."

"I'd love that, Daddy. It's been a while since we've seen Aunt Beck."

Melody was excited about the trip, but she couldn't help thinking of the playground project. She would be busy with the plants and flowers in June. Melody was the president, so it was her job to make sure everything got done properly. She put her fork down, wondering if a good leader would choose not to go see the farm.

Today is March eighth, Melody thought. *The Block Club picnic is August first. Even if I'm gone for a week, there will be enough time, when I get back, to get everything done.*

Melody relaxed. The farm meant a lot to her family, and she wasn't going to miss her chance to see it.

♫

"Poppa," Melody asked after dessert, "did you bring any of your seeds up here when you left Alabama?"

"Why, yes, and bulbs too. Those orange daylilies that

you like come from roots I brought. You know I call those great-great-grand—"

"—flowers," Melody finished, giggling. "Miss Esther gave me some heirloom seeds that came from her mother's garden," she explained. "Hollyhocks. I think I'd like to plant some along the playground fence, so she can see them from her window. They might remind her of where she came from."

Poppa gave Melody a kiss on top of her head. "I like the sound of that. On Friday, let's skip your work day at the flower shop and go take a look at that playground."

"That would be great!" Melody cried. "I'll ask Miss Esther and the Junior Block Club to meet us there."

As soon as school was out on Friday, Melody, Val, Diane, Sharon, and Julius raced to the park. While they waited for Melody's grandfather, Melody gave each person a copy of the playground wish list. She had spent all week writing out copies of the one she had made with Miss Esther, and now her friends were studying the pages.

Julius looked up from his copy. "Vegetables?" he asked. "Who plants vegetables in a playground?"

"Melody does," Val said loyally.

Diane shook her head. "I haven't even heard of some of the flowers on this list," she said.

"Me either," Sharon shrugged. "But Melody's the expert."

"No, my grandfather's the expert," Melody said. "And Miss Esther. She suggested some of these plants."

Julius grinned. "As long as the playground stuff gets fixed, I don't care what we grow."

"Here comes Miss Esther now," Sharon said.

The group turned to see Miss Esther crossing the street, her cane in one hand and a shoe box in the other.

Melody rushed to the curb. "Can I help you?" she asked, taking Miss Esther's elbow.

"Thank you, dear," Miss Esther said. "You may take this box. I thought you all might like a little snack after school."

Melody removed the lid. The box was lined with wax paper and filled with slices of banana bread. "Thank you!" she said, smiling.

When Poppa's truck rumbled to a stop in front of the park, the members of the Junior Block Club were all nibbling their second slices of bread. "Hello there," Poppa called. "I see you've started on the important business at hand."

Melody grinned and wiped the crumbs from her

hands. "Hi, Poppa." She gave him a copy of the playground wish list.

"Let's do it, then," Julius said, pushing open the creaking, squeaking gate and waving everyone into the park.

They all took a slow walk along the paths, talking about what needed to be done and checking the list to make sure everything was on it. Poppa and Miss Esther followed, asking questions.

They stopped at a jungle-like area near the jungle gym. "This is where we can plant flowers," Melody said, pointing to a stretch of snow-covered grass next to a tangle of overgrown bushes. "Something really colorful, so that when you're hanging upside down on the jungle gym, it looks like a rainbow!"

"My sisters will love that," Diane said.

"And more flowers there, and there . . ." Melody pointed with her pencil. She looked up at the sky and then spun around. "And since there's full sun over there, we could do vegetables. Right, Miss Esther?"

"You are right, Melody. Now you can draw all this up in your plan."

"Yes, ma'am," Melody said.

They all moved on to the peeling benches. "You'll need special paint for outdoors," Miss Esther said.

"What about these swings?" Poppa asked.

"I need to write to the Parks Commissioner about that," Melody said. Everybody says getting new swings is up to the city. If the Junior Block Club is going to work hard to clean up the playground, then it's only fair that we get some help. Kids are citizens, too!"

"That's exactly what you should say in your letter," Miss Esther told her.

Poppa nodded. "Now, do you have a budget?"

"You mean, money?" Diane said, looking at Melody.

Melody's stomach dropped. *Of course we'll need money,* she thought. She'd planned out everything except that.

"I suspect that our Block Club can provide some funds from our budget," Miss Esther said. "I'll bring it up at the next meeting."

Melody was relieved. "Thank you, Miss Esther."

Poppa nodded. "Some local businesses may be willing to donate supplies, too," he added.

Melody brightened. "I can dig up some plants from my garden this spring," she said. "That will save us some money."

"Now you're thinking," Sharon said.

Work Day

CHAPTER 8

April came, and it was warm enough for the Junior Block Club to start cleanup in the park. Poppa had given Melody some old gardening gloves from his workroom, and she had been saving paper grocery bags for trash, dead plants, and twigs. The club members had recruited some other neighborhood kids to help, and Melody had told everyone to wear long pants and long sleeves to the work day.

At nine o'clock on the second Saturday of the month, Melody and Val were the first to arrive at the park. Soon, Sharon came running up the block. A few minutes later, Mrs. Harris pulled up and Diane got out of the car.

"Where's everybody else?" Diane asked.

"I don't know," Sharon said.

Melody was concerned. She opened her notebook. "Well, I have the names of nine people who agreed to come. I wonder where Julius is."

"Here I am!" He walked across the street carrying two rakes. "I'm ready! I borrowed these from my dad."

"Good idea," Melody said, realizing that she hadn't

thought of bringing rakes. "So, where's everybody else?"

Julius looked around. "Larry and Clifton haven't shown up yet? They promised they'd come."

"Well, I guess we just have to get started," Melody said.

They went through the gate. The park looked pretty much the same as it had the last time they were there, except that the snow was gone. Melody put her box of supplies down on one of the benches. She realized that if everyone had shown up, she wouldn't have had enough gloves.

"Okay." Melody stood with her hands on her hips. "I say we each take a part of the park to work in. Let's call them zones. Julius, you take the handball zone. Sharon, how about you and Val in the swing zone? Diane, do you want to clear the flower beds with me?"

"Nah, I'm not much of a gardener," Diane said. "Sharon, switch with me?"

Sharon shook her head. "No, thanks."

Melody looked at Diane. *Is there a problem?* she thought. *Already?*

"I'll switch," Val said.

"Deal." Diane nodded.

Thank goodness, Melody thought. Everyone went to their zones, and Melody used one of Julius's rakes to show Val how to carefully clear the layers of dead leaves without damaging anything growing underneath.

As Val got started, Melody put her transistor radio on a bench and turned it on. "Work goes faster with music," she said, pulling the antenna all the way out. But after a few minutes, the only station that came in clearly was a talk show that no one wanted to listen to.

"We could sing," Diane suggested. "Then you wouldn't have to run down the battery on your radio." She started. *"If I had a hammer, I'd hammer in the morning . . ."*

Val burst out laughing. "We're not doing construction work!"

"Not yet," Julius said, picking up the song. *"I'd hammer in the evening, all over this* ***park****!"*

He'd changed the last word, and the rest of the kids giggled. Then they all joined in.

I'd hammer out danger,
I'd hammer out a warning,
I'd hammer out love between my brothers
and my sisters,
All over this land!

But after an hour, Sharon and Diane had quit working and had started climbing on the jungle gym. Everyone was hot from working—and playing—so the group took a break. Everyone was thirsty, too, but no one had brought anything to drink.

"Are we done for the day?" Diane asked, plopping down on one of the worn benches.

"I'm hungry," Julius said. "I'm going to head home."

"I have to go, too," Sharon said. "My mom's taking me to buy new shoes. Sorry, Melody," she called as she took off running.

Melody sat down next to Diane and sighed. She was sweaty and dirty and thirsty, and the Junior Block Club hadn't gotten as much done as she'd hoped they would. That's when Melody saw her grandfather's truck.

"Well, there," Poppa said, strolling through the gate carrying a large paper bag. "You all look a bit wilted." He set the bag down on the bench and pulled out a thermos and a stack of paper cups. "How about some water?"

"Thanks, Mr. Porter," Diane and Julius said.

Val joined them, and they all drank the water Poppa poured. Melody hoped Diane and Julius would stay, but after a few minutes, they both left.

Val went back to raking. Melody set her cup down and began to clap the dirt off her gloves. "Boy, this didn't go the way I thought," she mumbled.

"How did you think things would go?" Poppa asked, sitting down beside her.

Melody shook her head. "I thought because I knew about gardening that I'd be a better leader. But I didn't check to make sure everyone would show up. I didn't remember to bring tools. I didn't even bring water!"

"You're learning to be a leader, Little One," Poppa told her. "And being a leader doesn't mean you have to do everything yourself. Julius remembered tools. Why don't you make him head of the tool committee?"

"Really?" Melody asked. "I could do that?"

"Yes. And you could ask someone to remind the Junior Block Club members when there's a work day."

"Diane would love that," Val piped up. "She's good at being bossy."

"I guess," Melody said slowly. "But if other people do things, doesn't that mean I'm not a leader?"

"This is a big project, and you need many hands," Poppa said. "A good leader helps everyone see that they're a special part of the team. Leading takes patience, just like gardening. And you're right. You're a wonderful gardener. You know how to make things take root and grow. As your club works together, it will become stronger."

Melody nodded. "You make it sound like the Junior Block Club might blossom one day, Poppa."

"Won't it?" he asked.

Melody smiled. She sure hoped so.

Singing Together

CHAPTER 9

Talking to Poppa made Melody feel better. She went home and changed her clothes. She was about to get a snack from the kitchen when the phone rang.

Mommy called from the bathroom upstairs. "Melody, can you answer that, please?"

Melody picked up the phone. "Hello?"

"Hey, Dee-Dee." It was Dwayne. "I finally got that studio time. Are you ready to—"

"Sing with you?"Melody finished with excitement in her voice.

"Well, sing *for* me. For us. Sing backup. We're finally going to cut our own single." Melody heard the excitement in her brother's voice, too.

"Can Val come? And Sharon? And Lila? Just to watch?"

"Hey, it's not a stage show, all right? I'll find out. Anyway, Mom or Dad needs to bring you, and one of them has to sign something so that you can work in the studio. I'm gonna copy the lyrics and music and bring them home. You need to be at Motown at four o'clock tomorrow."

"Tomorrow?!" Melody gasped. "First, it's Sunday.

Second, I can't learn a new song by tomorrow! You want me to mess it up?"

Dwayne laughed. "You won't mess up. But I can only get into the studio when they tell me I can. Listen, you check with Mom, see if it's okay."

As soon as Dwayne clicked off, Melody ran upstairs shouting, "Mommy! Mommy!"

"Is the house on fire?" her father mumbled, opening their bedroom door. Melody rushed in.

"No, Daddy. Sorry. Dwayne just asked me to sing backup on his record! Can I? I can't do it without your permission. Please, please!"

Melody's mother opened the bathroom door across the hall. "How wonderful! Will, this would be a great opportunity for Melody. She could see the real work behind the flash."

"Don't try to get me on Dwayne's side, Frances," Melody's father answered. "I still believe a black man can have a better life with a college education. Not a record." Then Daddy looked at Melody. His face softened. "But for you? This sounds like a once-in-a-lifetime chance." He tugged Melody's pigtail. "You may go."

♫

Dwayne was as good as his word. That evening he came home with a handwritten copy of music and lyrics, a tape recorder, and a tape. If Daddy hadn't gone bowling,

Melody knew he would have been there, grilling Dwayne.

Mommy came downstairs. "This is so exciting, Dwayne! What an opportunity!"

"Thanks, Mom," Dwayne said.

"May I see the lyrics?" Mommy asked.

"Sure, Mom." Dwayne handed the sheet to his mother. "It's called 'Move On Up.' It's a good song for Melody."

Melody stuck her chin over her mother's shoulder to look, too. It was the song Dwayne had sung to her on her birthday. Melody stepped back, feeling even more excited.

"This is very nice, Dwayne," Mommy finally said. "I like the positive message."

Dwayne ducked his head, and Melody could see that he looked pleased. "I really didn't think of it like that. It just came into my head, and I wrote it." He handed Melody the cassette tape. "Melody, listen to this and follow along in the music. You'll see where I want you to come in. Let's try it."

Dwayne flipped the tape recorder on, and everyone was absolutely still. Melody had to concentrate very hard to focus on the music instead of her heart, which was pounding with excitement.

♫

At four the next afternoon, a carload of girls and one mom spilled out onto the sidewalk of West Grand Boulevard. Motown's Hitsville U.S.A. studio looked like an ordinary house except for the big display window in front. It was full of posters advertising performances by various Motown artists. Dwayne met the group at the door, looking very grown-up and serious.

"Is Mr. Gordy here?" Mommy asked.

"He lives upstairs, and he'll probably come down later. Right now it's just us. I'll give you a tour before Phil and Artie and the studio musicians arrive."

Dwayne led them through a maze of rooms, explaining what went on in each of them. As Dwayne talked about the songwriters and the people who designed the album covers, Melody began to realize that there was more to making a record than just singing.

The group went down a hallway, up a few steps, and then down a few others, and into a large room whose walls were covered with something that looked like a bulletin board. "Here's the studio," Dwayne said proudly.

"What's that on the walls?" Sharon asked.

"Soundproofing," Dwayne answered. "That way, no car sounds or people's voices from outside can mess up the recording. This isn't really a fancy setup," he said. "But the sound that comes out of here is more than fancy."

There were drums and cymbals in one corner, and other instruments resting against the wall. At one end of the room was a huge piano. "That's a *grand* piano,"

Mommy whispered. "Can you play a little something for us, Dwayne?" Mommy asked.

Dwayne sat on the bench and positioned his hands over the keys. Melody slid onto the seat beside him. Dwayne began to play a fast Motown-sounding tune. Melody moved her shoulders to the music as Dwayne sang.

Let me tell you about this girl
With a smile I know.
She's as happy as the crowd
At a carnival show.

Dwayne nudged Melody and grinned. "*That's why she's my very special Melody,*" he sang.

"Are you singing about *me*?" Melody asked. She looked at Sharon and Val, who were clapping along.

Dwayne grinned. "Why yes I am."

Melody noticed a small window that looked down on the room. There were people behind the glass. "What's that?" she asked. "Who's up there?"

"That's the control room," he said. "Those are the sound engineers, and they hear everything." Dwayne got up and crossed the room, motioning Melody to follow. "See these X's back here on the floor? This is where you'll stand. This microphone will be yours. Phil and Artie will be over here. I'll be at the piano."

Just then, Artie and Phil came into the studio. A moment later, a soft-spoken lady appeared. "Dwayne, may I take your guests upstairs now? The musicians are just about ready to start."

Mommy blew Melody a kiss before she and the girls followed the lady out.

Dwayne put his hand on Melody's shoulder and guided her to the X on the floor. "So, we're just gonna do this like we're hanging around in our backyard, got that?"

"Got it," Melody said.

The studio began to fill with the other musicians, who talked and laughed as they picked up their instruments. They didn't pay much attention to Melody. Most of them were much older than Dwayne. But when Dwayne sat down at the piano, Melody could tell that he became the leader. He wasn't bossy or rude. When he spoke, his voice was a man's voice, and the others listened.

"Fellas, we've changed this up a little bit from last time since our backup singer is here." He motioned toward Melody.

All the musicians turned to her with interest. Because of what Dwayne had said, the musicians thought of her as a real musician, too—not just a kid. Melody stood a little taller.

A voice filled the studio over a loudspeaker. It was coming from the control room. "Dwayne, Mr. Gordy wants to know if you're going to go right in, or riff a little first," the voice said.

"Riff, Mr. Gordy."

Berry Gordy is in there, Melody thought. *He's listening!*

Dwayne looked at Melody over the piano. "How're you feeling? Good?"

She nodded, and he began a jazzy tune, making it up as he went. Improvising, Big Momma called it. Melody felt herself moving to the rhythm.

"One. Two. One, two, three, four," Dwayne counted, and he was into the song. Melody closed her eyes, and when it was time, she sang. And sang. At the end of the second verse, Melody suddenly didn't hear Artie or Phil behind her, only Dwayne's piano. As he picked up the tempo of the music, Melody blinked her eyes open.

"Move on up," he sang, nodding at her.

"Move on up," Melody repeated, feeling happiness bubble up inside. She knew just what Dwayne was "calling," and it was her job to "respond" by singing whatever he sang in harmony. She'd heard the adult choir at church sing this way, and it always excited the congregation.

"Yeah, I'm movin'! I'm movin'!" Dwayne's fingers flew on the keys as he smiled at her.

"Yeah, I'm movin'! I'm movin'!" Melody sang back.

Dwayne threw one of his hands into the air while still

Melody sang and sang, feeling happiness bubble up inside.

playing smoothly with the other.

Artie's and Phil's voices came back in, singing, *"It's time to moooovvve."*

Dwayne hit the final notes, and then everything was still. After a moment, all the musicians cheered.

"That was something, Dwayne!"

"Hey, great. What a bunch of raw talent!"

"Man, that is going to be a hit!"

Melody danced toward her brother, still feeling the music. "Was I okay?" she asked.

"Not okay," he said.

Melody stopped dancing, but Dwayne pulled her into a bear hug. "You were perfect, Dee-Dee. And you made our record perfect, too."

Melody spun around. The musicians were clapping. She glanced up at the window of the sound booth and saw her mother and sister and friends clapping and waving. The other people in the booth looked pleased.

As she looked around, she wondered how many wonderful, talented singers had stood in this very place, on that same X. Melody didn't think she'd ever be a professional singer, and she would never be famous. But she loved singing, and she knew that she'd helped Dwayne get a little closer to his dream. She was overjoyed at that.

Constraints

CHAPTER 10

On the following Saturday, Melody arrived at the playground pulling her old red wagon. In it were a thermos of water, some paper cups, a box of graham crackers, and a bag of apples. At the gate, she met Julius and a couple of his friends. They were carrying armloads of gardening tools. She smiled as Julius gave her a thumbs-up.

"Hi, Melody!" Diane greeted her just inside the park. "I took attendance today. We have two third-graders, five fourth-graders, and two sixth-graders, plus Val, Sharon, and Julius. I called everyone yesterday to remind them."

"Thanks, Diane," Melody said. "You made sure we have plenty of hands for our work day." Melody rolled the wagon near one of the benches. Her grandfather had been right, again. Once she asked her friends to do the things they were good at, they were even more interested in working on the work days. Now Melody could concentrate on the garden plan.

"Good morning, everybody!" Melody called out.

"Morning, Melody!" everyone shouted back. But no one stopped working.

Melody walked around the paths, noticing where tiny new plants were breaking through the earth in the spring sun. She pulled out her pad and pencil to make notes, humming Dwayne's new song as she went. Soon, everyone else had picked up the tune and was humming along with her, without even knowing the words.

As Melody passed her, Val whispered, "Good job getting publicity for Dwayne's record!"

Melody grinned. "Wait until they hear the real thing!"

♫

After school on Monday, Val came home with Melody. The girls went to the kitchen for a snack, and there on the table was a long white envelope addressed to Melody. It had a seal with the words "City of Detroit" in the corner.

"I bet it's an answer from the Parks Commissioner!" Val said. "Finally! Open it!"

"We're going to get our swings!" Melody said with excitement. She read the letter to Val.

April 17, 1964

Dear Miss Ellison,

We regret to inform you that due to budget constraints, the Parks Department will not be able to replace the swings in your neighborhood park. Thank you for being a concerned citizen.

Melody stopped reading. She couldn't believe it. "They said no."

"What's a constraint?" Val asked.

"I'm not sure," Melody said. "But it can't be good." She was angry. "They thank me for being a concerned citizen, but they won't help? That's not fair."

Val shook her head. "What are we going to do now?"

"Meet with the Junior Block Club," Melody said. "Right away."

♫

Melody called an emergency meeting that afternoon, and everyone gathered at Miss Esther's house. Melody read the letter out loud.

"This is so unfair," Sharon said.

Diane nodded. "It's wrong. Do you think the Parks Department said no because the park is in a black neighborhood?"

The kids looked at one another. "That doesn't make any sense," Melody said. She turned to Miss Esther, who hadn't said anything yet. "Is that why?"

"That's an important question," Miss Esther said thoughtfully. "Sometimes Negro neighborhoods don't get the same services as other neighborhoods. Trash isn't picked up as often, and potholes don't get repaired as quickly. One of the reasons we have a Block Club is to ask these sorts of questions. We have to call attention to things that aren't right and then figure out how to fix them."

The group was quiet, and Melody could see that everyone was as disappointed as she was.

"So how do we fix this?" Julius finally asked. "This is our big Challenge project and we can't even do it."

"That's not entirely true," Miss Esther said gently. "You can't do everything you want all at once, but you have already accomplished quite a bit."

Melody remembered something Miss Esther had said back when they first talked about the park cleanup. "Miss Esther's right," Melody told the Junior Block Club. "New swings were on our wish list, but we didn't get them. That doesn't mean we give up. It means we change our plan."

"Okay," said Julius. "What's the new plan?"

"There's still a bunch of stuff to clean up," Diane said.

"We haven't painted the benches yet," Val added.

"And we have a lot of planting to do," Melody said. "Let's keep working. How many can meet after school tomorrow?"

Everyone raised their hands, including Miss Esther.

"Good," Melody said, feeling hopeful again.

♫

After school the next day, Melody and her friends hurried home to change their clothes. On her way to the park,

Melody stopped at her grandparents' house to get Val, and the two of them headed to the playground.

When they turned the corner, Melody saw everyone from yesterday's meeting standing outside the gate. *What are they waiting for?* she wondered.

When Sharon started to run toward her, Melody knew that something was wrong.

"What is it?" Melody said when Sharon got to her side.

"Come and see." Sharon pulled her to the park entrance. The gate was closed, and on it was a big fat padlock.

Melody gasped. "What happened?" she asked.

"Read that," Julius said angrily, pointing to a sign posted on the gate.

"Closed by the Parks Department," Melody read. "What

does that mean? Closed for today? For the weekend?"

"I don't know," Julius said, "but it stinks."

Miss Esther was making her way across the street. "Hello, children," she called wearily. "I saw a truck from the city pull up this morning. The inspector walked all around the park, and he looked at the broken swing. I believe he thought it was dangerous. That's when he put a lock on the gate."

"But why would he close the whole park?" Melody asked. "The swing's been like that forever! Didn't he see all the work we've done?"

Diane nodded. "They could have just taken that swing away and let us keep everything else."

Melody was disappointed, but she was also angry. There was no other playground close enough to walk to in their neighborhood.

"Now what?" Julius asked.

Melody had no idea.

More Letters

CHAPTER 11

Melody could hardly pay attention in school the next day. All she could think about was the lock on the gate. Miss Esther had suggested that the Junior Block Club write several letters to the Parks Commissioner. "The more letters he gets, the more likely he is to listen," Miss Esther had told them. Everyone had agreed to write, but Melody hadn't started her letter yet. It didn't seem as though the city was going to help a bunch of kids, after all.

When Melody got home, she'd gotten a letter of her own, from Yvonne. Melody took it up to her room, flipped on her radio, and listened to The Supremes while she read.

April 18, 1964
Dear Melody,

I had my interview for the Summer Project in Mississippi. It went well, and I really hope I get accepted. Now that I know more about the program, I've decided I want to volunteer with the Freedom Schools. It will be a lot of work—especially since I've never taught before. (Unless you count the fact that I taught Lila everything she knows about hair. Ha ha.)

But you know what? You've inspired me. You took on the playground project even though you've never done anything like it before. You're my role model, Dee-Dee. Pretty soon everybody's going to be talking about the park and all the work you and your friends have done. Keep me posted on all your progress.

Love, Vonnie

Melody couldn't believe it. Yvonne thought *she* was a role model? Her brave, smart, strong big sister was inspired by what Melody was doing? For a moment, Melody was flattered. Then she sighed. Yvonne didn't know that the Junior Block Club was locked out of the park. What would Yvonne say if she knew about that "progress"?

The song on the radio ended, and a woman's voice filled Melody's room. "This is Martha Jean the Queen." Melody loved her smooth voice. Martha Jean Steinberg was one of the most popular DJs in Detroit. Any song she played became a hit, and anything she discussed on her show was what grown-ups all over the city talked about. Melody imagined the Queen one day introducing Dwayne's music. Everyone in Detroit would be singing his song.

Wait a minute, Melody thought. She reread Yvonne's

letter. *"Pretty soon everybody's going to be talking about the park and all the work you and your friends have done."* If more people knew that the city had closed the park, maybe they would write to the commissioner, too.

Melody needed help letting others know about the problem. She got a clean piece of paper and a pencil. "Dear Miss Steinberg," she began.

A week passed, and the lock was still on the park gate. Melody was worried that every day they spent not working on the playground meant they were getting further and further away from having the park done in time for the picnic. They hadn't done any planting yet, and Melody was afraid that the garden wouldn't be ready.

At dinner that night, Melody picked at her food.

"Are you all right, Melody?" Mommy asked. "You haven't eaten much."

Melody shrugged. She was feeling very out of sorts.

"Is the park still locked?" Daddy asked.

Melody nodded her head. "Is this my fault?" she asked her parents. "I'm the one who told the Parks Department about the broken swing."

Mommy put her fork down and took Melody's hand in hers. "The lock on the park gate is not your fault. Even a good leader can't make everything go right."

Daddy nodded. "You got people to trust you and work with you. No way is that a failure, and no way is what happened your fault."

"Besides," Lila chimed in. "The Junior Block Club cleaned up the park. It looks a lot better than it did before."

"Thanks, everyone," Melody said. "I just miss working in the park."

"Well, you don't want to miss the latest Motown record!" Dwayne came in through the kitchen door waving a small black disc. "Here it is, for your ears only."

"It's out?" Lila cried.

"Let's hear it right now!" Melody shouted. She jumped up from her chair and raced to the record player. Dwayne slipped the record out of its paper sleeve, handed it to Melody, and let her place it on the turntable. She started the record player, and everyone listened.

Girl, it's time that I move,
Time for movin' on up.
Move on up!
Yeah, it's time for my move,
Time to start changing my luck.
Move on up!

When the song was over, Daddy pushed back his chair,

got up, and shook Dwayne's hand. "I'm proud of you, son," he said, his voice full of emotion. "You did what you set out to do. Keep on doing it."

Melody and Val were washing the dishes in Big Momma's kitchen after lunch on Saturday. There was a commercial on the radio, and when it was over, Martha Jean the Queen came on the air. "God bless you and I love you!" she said. Martha Jean started all of her broadcasts with those words.

Tish stopped talking and turned toward the kitchen. "Oh, I love the Queen's program! She plays the best music, and she brings up such interesting topics."

"Turn up the sound, girls," Big Momma said.

Martha Jean's voice got louder. "Let's give our support to a group of children from New Hope Baptist Church who banded together to do something special for their community. They asked the Parks Department for new swings. Not only did they get turned down, but they got locked out of their playground! It's a shame that the city and our wonderful mayor can't help these children who have worked *so* hard to improve their neighborhood. Call in if you agree."

"That's us!" Val said. "How did she know?"

Melody grinned. "I wrote another letter. But this time

I sent it to someone who would talk about our park."

"Melody to the rescue," Big Momma said.

♫

On the last Thursday in May, Melody received another long white envelope with the city seal in the corner. She tore it open and let out a shriek of joy. Melody called Sharon, Val, Diane, and Julius and asked them to meet her at the park right away.

When Melody got to the park, everyone else was there. "Melody, look!" Julius shouted. "The lock's gone!"

"I know," Melody said. "Listen, everybody."

May 26, 1964

Dear Miss Ellison,

As a result of the many telephone calls and letters we have received about your local park, our inspectors have reviewed the conditions there. After removing the broken swing, we have determined that the park is safe for recreation. Thank you for being a good citizen.

"Let's get back to work!" Melody said, waving the letter in the air. She looked over at the yellow house. Miss Esther stood in the front window, smiling and waving.

♫

After the lock came off the gate, the Junior Block Club

sprang into action. That Saturday, a group of dads replaced the missing bricks in the walls of the handball courts with the help of Julius, Diane, and Sharon. While that was happening, Val, Melody, and Miss Esther planted more flowers. Poppa came and helped start the vegetable garden.

Things were looking good. On the next work day, Julius's older brother brought cans of paint and brushes. By then, some moms and kids were coming in to see everything, so Melody made big signs with leftover butcher paper that said: WET PAINT. Then it rained, so they had to do it all over again.

Whenever Melody went to the park to work, she took her transistor radio with her. And it was *always* tuned to Martha Jean the Queen's show.

Important Work

CHAPTER 12

The week before their trip to Alabama, Melody's father was watching television in the living room while Melody and her mother sat at the dining room table talking about what they needed to pack. "That reminds me, Will," Mommy said during a commercial. "Would you bring the suitcases up from the basement?"

"Will do!" Daddy answered, and Melody laughed at his favorite joke. "I'll go down after the news."

The commercial ended and a newscaster said, "In national news today, the search continues for three young civil rights workers who are missing in Mississippi."

"What?" Daddy said.

"Mississippi?" Melody repeated. "That's where Yvonne is going," she said in a small voice. Earlier that month, Yvonne had called home to tell them she'd been accepted to the Mississippi Summer Project. Instead of coming home when her college classes were finished, she was going to Ohio for training.

Mommy got up and went into the living room. Melody followed.

"According to CORE, the Congress for Racial Equality, James Chaney, 21, Andrew Goodman, 20, and Michael Schwerner, 24, were investigating the burning of a Negro church in the area. CORE members say the men were arrested on June twenty-first without cause, held in jail for several hours, and then released. The trio has not been seen or heard from since."

Melody felt the same knot in her tummy that she'd felt when she heard about the four little girls who had died in the church bombing in Birmingham.

"Oh, my goodness," Mommy said.

"Do you think they're all right?" Melody asked.

Mommy shook her head. "I don't know, Melody."

Melody tried to make sense of what she'd just heard. It frightened her to think that civil rights workers could just disappear. Then Melody had a horrible thought. "Do you think *Vonnie* is all right?" she asked.

"I pray she is safe," Mommy said. But she looked very concerned.

"There's one way to find out," Daddy said, getting up. "Where's her phone number, Frances?"

"By the phone, on the yellow paper," Mommy answered. She and Melody followed him to the kitchen.

Daddy picked up the phone and dialed. "Hello?" he said. "Yes, this is Will Ellison, Yvonne Ellison's father. I'd like to speak to her, please."

Melody stood beside her mother, waiting to hear that Yvonne was okay. The seconds seemed to tick by slowly. Daddy tapped impatiently on the telephone receiver. Melody could tell that he was nervous, too.

"Yvonne!" Daddy finally said. He looked at Melody and smiled. Mommy sighed.

"How's everything going?" Daddy asked. He began to nod. "We just heard about that on the news."

Melody turned to her mother. "Do you want Vonnie to come home?" she asked.

Mommy shook her head. "Even if I did, Melody, Yvonne is a strong person, and she makes her own choices now. The work she's decided to do is very important, but the struggle for justice isn't easy. Your sister is becoming a grown-up."

Mommy pulled Melody into a hug. "Mothers and fathers always hope that their children will be safe and make good choices, no matter how old they are. We hope that for all of you."

Melody's tummy settled down. Yvonne was brave and strong and smart, and Melody knew she would make good choices.

Standing Tall

CHAPTER 13

We're going to pass Birmingham and go straight to the farm," Poppa told the girls. "I want to see it before nightfall."

Melody was stiff from sitting in the car for so long. The trip had taken almost twelve hours. They had left Detroit long before sunrise so that they could get to Alabama in the daylight.

Poppa turned off the paved highway and onto a dirt road. They drove for another hour. Melody was surprised when Poppa slowed down next to an empty field, turned onto a rutted path, and stopped the car. Without saying a word, he and Melody's mother got out.

Val looked at Melody, confused. "This looks like no-where," she said, not moving.

Melody nodded, but she stumbled out to stretch.

Although she'd never been here before, there was something that felt familiar to Melody. Maybe it was the wildflowers dotting the field with shades of yellow and bright blue. They reminded her of the flowers in her own yard as well as the garden at the park. *I hope Sharon and*

Diane remember to water everything, Melody thought.

"Poppa?" Melody called. "When will we get to your old farm?"

Her grandfather didn't answer. He'd stopped to stare off at something Melody and Val couldn't see.

Melody's mother turned to them. "This is it," she said.

Melody looked around in surprise. There were no trees. There was no beautiful flower garden surrounded by the wooden fence Poppa had built. In fact, nothing here was the way her grandparents had described. All Melody could see was a dusty path cutting through the grass.

Melody walked over to her grandfather and tugged on his sleeve. "Is it gone?"

Poppa shook his head. "No. It's here," he said, bending to scoop up a handful of dirt. He let the dirt run through his fingers. "You're standing on it. Standing on the shoulders of all our people who came before."

Melody looked down at her dusty sandals, imagining her grandfather as a boy, and his parents, and maybe even their parents, walking on this same path. She looked up at Poppa, and tried to stand just a little bit taller than she had before.

Melody's mother and grandfather began to walk, and the girls followed in the late afternoon heat. The road curved, and Poppa pointed. In the distance was an old building, and beyond it another field.

"Is that your house?" Melody asked her mother.

"No," her mother said. "Aunt Beck told us that a tree fell on the house during a storm about ten years ago. The house was too damaged to repair, so what was left was torn down."

"That's awful," Melody said, frowning.

"So what's that building, then?" Val asked.

"I think it's the old barn," Mommy said.

"That's just what it is," Poppa said in a firm voice. He started walking toward it.

They all followed the rough road. The wildflowers ended, and there was a rickety wood and wire fence on either side of the path. "Doesn't look like anyone's farmed the land in a long while," Poppa said. "I guess the fellow I sold to ended up selling, too. It's a shame." Poppa shook his head. "This was such rich land."

The road ended in a gravel clearing, and the barn sat in the middle of it. The girls stopped and watched Poppa try the door. It didn't budge. He walked the length of the front, peering in through two dusty windows.

"It looks sad," Val whispered. Melody agreed.

"Everything is different," Mommy said.

"This way, girls!" Poppa called, heading past the barn. Despite the heat, he walked quickly.

Melody, Val, and Mommy hurried to follow Poppa. When they rounded the barn, Melody saw a broad grin stretch across Poppa's face, making his silver mustache twitch.

"Well, I'll be!" Melody's mother said. "The pecan trees!"

"There's some farm left, after all," Poppa said.

"Did you plant them all?" Melody asked.

"My father and I did," Poppa said. He smiled at Melody. "Just like you and I plant tomatoes every year."

Melody smiled, too. "Tradition," she whispered.

They all walked a long way through tall grass to reach the trees. The tree trunks were fat, gnarled, and gray, but their branches stretched up and spread wide across the sky.

"My pecan trees," Poppa said, touching one of the trunks.

"Melody," her mother said. "You and Val go over and stand with Poppa so I can get a picture."

The grass tickled Melody's legs as she ran toward her grandfather. He put one arm around Melody's shoulders and another around Val's. Just before Mommy snapped the photo, Melody reached out to rub her hand against the pecan tree.

♫

It was nightfall by the time they drove back into Birmingham, to the little green house where Poppa's sister,

Aunt Beck, lived. They'd just gotten out of the car when Aunt Beck threw open her screen door. Her long silver braid was wound neatly around her head, and her eyeglasses were perched on her nose.

"I declare, Frank! What took you so long? I've had supper waiting for these babies"—she paused to squeeze Melody and Val in one tight hug—"for hours!" she continued. "Where have you been?"

Melody laughed at the idea of her grandfather having a big sister. When Poppa mumbled his answer, he sounded just like Dwayne talking to Yvonne.

Melody and Val both loved visiting Aunt Beck, and her living room was one reason why. Every table and shelf was covered with knickknacks. There were china figurines, tiny dolls, picture frames, and small glass candy dishes filled with an assortment of sweets. What Melody liked best was that Aunt Beck was not the type of adult who didn't allow kids to look at her special things. Aunt Beck happily let Melody and Val pick up anything they liked.

Poppa rolled his eyes as he tried to carry the suitcases through the room without knocking anything over.

"Look at all this stuff," Melody said, pointing at a table in the corner. "Everything has an American flag on it." She was impressed by the ceramic bald eagle carrying a flag in its beak.

"Well, the Fourth of July is only five days away," Val said.

Melody opened the top of a flag-shaped tin box. "Candy!" she said. She took a chocolate kiss and handed one to Val.

"Mmmm . . . it's good to be back in Birmingham," Val mumbled through a mouthful of chocolate.

♫

Melody liked the fact that members of the same family celebrated holidays differently. Back in Detroit, Daddy would be up early on the Fourth of July to start the barbecue. Here at Aunt Beck's, her son Clifford brought over barbecue in the afternoon. In the morning, Aunt Beck peeled peaches for her homemade ice cream.

Melody woke up early to help. But when she got to the kitchen, ready to work, Aunt Beck insisted she have something to eat first.

Melody sat at the kitchen table with a cinnamon bun and a glass of milk. Aunt Beck was humming a tune that Melody thought she recognized. "I know that song from school. It's 'America the Beautiful,' isn't it?" Melody started to sing, and so did Aunt Beck.

And crown thy good with brotherhood
From sea to shining sea.

"I think that's the most important part of the song, isn't it?" Aunt Beck said to Melody. "That brotherhood part. That's what we've all got to figure out."

Melody nodded, her mouth full of warm cinnamon bun. She and Aunt Beck talked about Yvonne and the Mississippi Summer Project, and then Melody told Aunt Beck about the Challenge to Change and her park project.

"Good for you kids," Aunt Beck said. "Now that President Johnson has signed the Civil Rights Act, I expect we'll see even more changes."

Melody nodded. "The law says that we're all equal, and have equal rights. That's what we've been marching for and protesting about all this time."

"Now we just have to get everybody to obey the law," Aunt Beck said.

In the afternoon, Aunt Beck's son Clifford, his wife, Katie, and their children and grandchildren arrived. The house was full. Melody didn't get many chances to spend time with little kids, and neither did Val—so they had great fun playing tag and peek-a-boo with their much younger cousins. At dusk, Clifford announced that it was time to go find spots to see the fireworks. Aunt Beck stayed home, but everyone else piled into cars.

Melody stood next to Val, speechless at the beauty of

the fireworks in the sky above a giant statue called *Vulcan*. She and Val argued all the way back about which city's celebration was better—Birmingham's or Detroit's.

"Hey, you live in Detroit now," Melody reminded Val. "So you have to be loyal!"

Clifford, a lawyer, looked at the girls in his rearview mirror. "I say Val can claim dual citizenship."

"What's that?" Melody asked.

"It means she can be a citizen of two places at the same time," Clifford told her. Melody folded her arms and pretended to be upset, while Val laughed.

When Clifford pulled into the driveway, Mommy said, "Now why does Aunt Beck have every light on in the house?"

Before anyone could venture a guess, Aunt Beck swung the front door open. Her braid hung against her back. She looked worried.

"Frances, Will has been calling and calling!"

"He has?" Melody's mother hurried out of the car and up the porch steps. "What's wrong?"

"It's Yvonne," Aunt Beck said. "She's been arrested in Mississippi."

Civil Rights

CHAPTER 14

Melody rushed into the house after Mommy. Val, Poppa, and Clifford followed. "You girls stay here," Poppa ordered before hurrying into the kitchen.

Melody and Val sat down in the living room. The TV was on, and Melody strained to hear what was happening in the kitchen. Her mother must have called home, because Melody heard Mommy say, "Will! Aunt Beck just told me. Have you heard from her? Not since when?"

Melody felt her lip tremble. She couldn't sit still, so she hurried into the kitchen. Val followed.

Mommy was on the phone, listening to Daddy. Melody crossed the room so she could be close to Mommy.

"What happened?" Clifford asked when Melody's mother hung up.

"Yvonne called home yesterday to say she'd been arrested for disturbing the peace. Will hasn't heard from her since, and he can't get any answers from the police station in someplace called Meridian."

"What do you want to do?" Poppa asked.

"Go find her!" Melody's mother said. Melody heard

determination in her mother's voice, but also fear.

Melody's heart was pounding, and her throat felt tight. All she could think of were the civil rights workers who had disappeared. Yvonne was a civil rights worker.

"Let me drive you," Clifford said. "You don't need to be in Mississippi with a Michigan license plate on your car, Uncle Frank. Some people over there look for any reason to cause trouble for black people."

"All right," Mommy said, grabbing her purse. "We need to go."

"I want to come with you," Melody said.

Mommy turned to Melody and squeezed her hand. "You'll have to stay here with Aunt Beck."

Then they were gone.

"Are you okay?" Val asked gently.

Melody only nodded. Her throat hurt, and she didn't feel like talking. Aunt Beck tried to convince her to sleep, but Melody couldn't. She was too worried. When both Aunt Beck and Val finally went to bed, Melody stayed up. She sat on the edge of the sofa in the living room, staring at the Fourth of July decorations on the coffee table.

She had so many thoughts crammed into her brain at once that she had a headache. *Is Yvonne okay? Is she missing, like those three civil rights workers who disappeared a few weeks ago?* Melody thought of Aunt Beck sounding so pleased that the Civil Rights Act was now a law. But what good was a law if it couldn't keep people safe?

Melody leaned back against the sofa. She tried to focus her thoughts on the pecan trees at Poppa's old farm, standing strong and tall during a bad storm.

♫

Melody dreamed that her sisters were calling to her across a field of tall grass. "Melody? Melody!"

She opened her eyes to sunlight streaming through Aunt Beck's living room windows. Melody had fallen asleep on the sofa, and now Yvonne was sitting next to her, calling her name.

"Vonnie!" Melody blinked to make sure her sister was real. Yvonne looked tired. Her Afro was tied back with a scarf, and her left wrist was bandaged.

Melody carefully threw her arms around Yvonne. "Are you okay?" she asked, squeezing her sister tightly.

"I'm all right," Yvonne said, squeezing back. "I got banged up a little, that's all. I'll tell you everything, I promise. But right now, I need to sleep."

♫

Yvonne slept into the afternoon and woke up in time to have dinner. "You sit right down here, baby," Aunt Beck said to Yvonne, pulling out a chair at the kitchen table. Clifford joined Melody and Val while Poppa said grace.

Melody carefully threw her arms around Yvonne.
"Are you okay?" she asked, squeezing her sister tightly.

"Thanks, Mom," Yvonne said as Mommy placed a plate of food in front of her. She picked up her fork with her right hand, and because she was left-handed, she had trouble using it.

"Can I help?" Melody asked quietly.

Yvonne nodded. "Gee, thanks, Dee-Dee."

Melody picked up her sister's knife. "Vonnie," Melody said gently. "What happened?"

"Well," Yvonne began, watching Melody cut her meat into pieces. "It's not all that complicated. We had our training and orientation in Oxford, Ohio. That's where I learned to work with elementary school kids, helping improve their reading skills. We also got instructions to be calm when we got arrested."

Melody noticed that Yvonne said "when," not "if."

Yvonne continued. "When we got to Mississippi—to Meridian—we went out to invite black parents to send their kids to our Freedom School. There were four of us: two white college students, me, and a black high school boy who lived in the area."

"That was good," Aunt Beck said. "You were with somebody the people knew."

"Yes, exactly," Yvonne said. "So we were on the front porch of a house, and this family, the teenagers and parents, were really interested in talking to us. They were asking all kinds of questions. That's when the sheriff's car pulled up along the road. No siren, no flashing lights. I don't even know why he was there."

"Was that scary?" Melody asked.

Yvonne took a deep breath. "Yes. But all of us knew what would happen. That part was in our training, too. The sheriff came up and told us that we were disturbing the peace. The man who owned the house was brave enough to tell the sheriff that he *wanted* to talk to us. But the sheriff repeated that we were disturbing the peace and said we were under arrest."

Mommy shook her head. "That's worse than getting turned away at a hotel or restaurant. Those people have a right to talk to whomever they want. And so do you."

"Yes, but the law enforcement in Mississippi is not interested in giving any black people any kind of civil rights," Clifford said.

Yvonne nodded. "The sheriff dragged us off the porch. As he was pulling me, I tripped on the steps. He kept pulling me anyway, and I fell and broke my wrist. He still took us to jail."

"That's horrible!" Val said.

Yvonne turned to Mommy. "I did get my one phone call. I called home and Lila answered. I told her to tell you and Dad that I was okay. I know that those three freedom workers are still missing, and I knew that everyone would be worried about me." Yvonne stopped because her voice got shaky. Melody put her hand on her sister's.

Yvonne smiled at Melody, and then she took a deep breath. She looked defiant. "I knew my rights, but I didn't know if I would get out of jail. I didn't know if I would ever come home. But now I know that I am not going to stop fighting for freedom."

"I want you to keep fighting," Mommy said. "But I want you to take care of yourself, too. You need to take a break and get yourself together."

Yvonne shook her head. "No, Mom. I want to go back."

Mommy put her fork down. "Yvonne, I don't know if—"

Melody interrupted. "Mommy, didn't you say that Yvonne was old enough to make her own choices?"

Everyone was quiet, and Mommy gave Melody a long look. Mommy sighed. "I did say that."

"I'll be as careful as I can," Yvonne said, "but we all know the fight isn't over. President Johnson just signed the Civil Rights Act, but this fight is not on paper."

Aunt Beck cleared her throat. "Yvonne, why don't you stay here for a few days to rest up? Then Clifford can take you back to Mississippi."

"Thanks, Aunt Beck. I'll stay if Mommy agrees to let me go back to Mississippi."

"Frances," Clifford said to Mommy, "if it makes you feel any better, I have friends in Meridian who can keep an eye on her."

Mommy nodded. "It does. But let me talk to Will about it tonight. For now, let's enjoy being with one another. All right?"

"That sounds fine," Aunt Beck said. "Now, I've got peach cobbler just waiting to get eaten up!"

Yvonne leaned toward Melody. "Thanks," she said.

"You're welcome," Melody answered.

♫

For the next few days, Melody didn't leave Yvonne's side. She helped Yvonne do anything she couldn't do because of her injured wrist. Yvonne rested a lot, but she and Melody talked a lot, too. Melody told her all about the trip to the Motown studio and how amazing it had been to see Dwayne as a real musician. She described Poppa's farm and how different it looked from what she expected. Yvonne asked Melody lots of questions about her park project, and she was impressed that Melody had thought to write a letter to Martha Jean the Queen. "That's makin' it work, Dee-Dee," she'd said.

Daddy had agreed that Yvonne could go back to Meridian on the condition that she call home every few days. So early on Thursday morning, everyone left

Birmingham at the same time. Melody walked Yvonne to Clifford's car.

"I know this has been scary for you," Yvonne said, gesturing to the bandage on her wrist, "but I'm glad we got a chance to see each other."

"Me, too," Melody said. "I'm glad you're okay."

"I am okay. And I'm not doing this alone. Neither are you, Dee-Dee," Yvonne said gently. "Remember. You came up with a great plan for the park, and you found great kids to work with. Trust them."

"Okay," Melody promised as Yvonne got in the car.

"And don't forget to send me pictures of that playground!" Yvonne yelled as Clifford pulled away.

Keep Going

CHAPTER 15

When they got back to Detroit that night, Poppa drove them all to his house, where Big Momma had a meal waiting. Val's parents were there, and Daddy and Lila had come over for supper, too. Even Dwayne joined them. Everyone wanted to hear about the trip.

"So, Frances," Charles said, sitting down at the dining room table, "what happened with Yvonne?"

"I kind of want to know the answer to that question, too," Dwayne said, looking at his mother. "Is she safe down there?"

"I admit, I've been worried about Yvonne ever since I heard the news reports about those three young men who went missing," Big Momma said, folding her hands together.

Tish shook her head. "I just don't think we could ever allow Valerie to do something like what Yvonne is doing."

"Wait a minute," Daddy said. "We all care about our children, and we care about the world they grow up in, don't we?"

Charles nodded. "That's true, Will."

Tish nodded, too. She started to say something else, but Mommy put both her hands in the air.

"Listen, everyone. We have a freedom fighter. Her name is Yvonne Marie Ellison. She has decided to go where we will not go—" Mommy looked at Melody. "Or cannot yet go, to lift her voice and use her gifts to try to make the world better for all of us. Every day there are black people and white people putting themselves in harm's way to change the world." Mommy's voice was shaking. "And I am so very, very proud of my Yvonne!"

Daddy got up, walked around the table, and put his arm around Mommy's shoulders. "Ditto," was all he said.

"Wow. Mom and Dad have got Yvonne's back," Dwayne whispered to Lila. Lila nodded.

Melody was so very, very proud of all of them.

♫

Melody was up early the next morning, and she dressed quickly so that she could go check on the play-ground. She was anxious to see how everything looked after her time away. As they rounded the corner by the park, Melody's heart beat fast. She saw the tall stems of the hollyhocks and daylilies standing at attention. The morning sun had already opened many of the lilies' orange flowers, and the hollyhocks looked like bright red ruffles.

As she swung the park gate open, Melody did a double

take. It didn't creak! Someone had oiled the hinges.

To her surprise, Diane and Sharon were already at work in the vegetable patch.

"Hi!" Melody called out.

"Hey, Melody." Diane pushed back the sun hat she was wearing. Behind her was a tall bamboo tepee with green-bean vines carefully wound around each slender stick.

"Nice beans," Melody said.

Diane grinned. "I've kind of started to like gardening," she said. "Look! The beans have *flowers* on them!" She pointed to the tiny white blossoms.

"Yes, they do," Melody said. "We—I mean, you—will have green beans soon. That's great!"

"Take a look around and check things out," Sharon said. "We've been working really hard."

Melody was pleased to see that the flower beds had been weeded and watered. The red geraniums were perky, and the tiny impatiens looked like mounds of orange, pink, and white popcorn. It was still disappointing not to have swings, but all the flowers made Melody happy.

"It's looking good, huh?"

Melody turned to see Julius and his friend Larry. Julius was wearing gardening gloves. "Welcome back," he said. "Larry and I just stopped by to do a little weeding."

Melody saw that Larry was carrying a ball.

"Well, we want to break in the handball courts before the opening," Julius said with a shrug.

Melody laughed. "It looks great. I can't wait for the picnic, so everyone can see what we've done."

"Three weeks and counting!" Julius said, heading off with Larry.

Melody wrote down a few things in her notebook. There were some bare spots in the flower border in back, and she wanted to get some plants to fill them in. And the hopscotch grids hadn't been painted on the paths yet. Other than that, all they had to do was keep weeding, pinch back the dead blooms so the plants continued to flower, and make sure everything was watered.

"Not bad," she said as she turned to leave. "Not bad at all!"

In church the Sunday before the picnic, Pastor Daniels made an announcement. "Some of our fine young people have answered the New Year's challenge with good works."

He made Melody and her friends stand up in front of the congregation. "I asked them to use their gifts to make justice, equality, and dignity grow," Pastor Daniels went on. "They did so by making an entire *garden* grow! Well done, Junior Block Club." Everyone applauded, and Melody and her friends beamed.

On Monday evening, Melody went over plans with Mr. Sterling, who was on the picnic planning committee. Every year, the club got permission from the city to close off a block to traffic. Neighbors set up tables and grills and brought food to share. Sometimes there was music, and this year The Three Ravens were going to perform.

Tuesday started out bright and sunny as Melody headed over to the park with Bo and a wagon full of marigolds that Poppa had given her to fill in the bare spots. Sharon was there to paint the hopscotch grids, and Diane was checking the vegetables. They all sang and hummed while they worked.

By the time Melody headed home, the sky had turned cloudy. "Looks like rain, Bo," she said, scooping him up into the wagon and running. "Let's move fast." Bo barked as the wagon bumped along the sidewalk. They made it home just as the rain began to pelt down.

Mommy was reading when Melody came in. "How's the garden?" she asked, sipping her coffee.

"Perfect," Melody said, wiping her wet sneakers on the doormat. "And the rain is just what all the plants need to look great this weekend."

Melody didn't know that the rain would turn into a storm.

Lila stomped in soaking wet, and later their father came

home from work the same way. Daddy went to bed early, as usual, but Mommy stayed up with Melody and Lila and played board games. They listened to Dwayne's record over and over and tried to ignore the thunder.

But the fun didn't keep Melody from worrying about the weather. It rained through the night and all the next day. The wind blew and the rain pounded. On the second night there was lightning.

By Thursday morning the storm had passed. When Melody turned on her radio, the weatherman was saying that there might have been a tornado.

"A tornado? In Detroit?" Lila mumbled sleepily. "What is he talking about?"

Melody hopped out of bed and went to the window. "Well, I see a huge branch down in the yard behind ours, and the lawn chairs are all over the place. I hope the playground is okay," she said, getting dressed quickly.

Melody hurried downstairs to find her mother and grandfather sitting at the kitchen table.

"Where are you off to?" Mommy asked.

"I want to make sure everything at the garden and playground is all right," Melody said.

"Why don't I go with you," Poppa said, putting on his cap. "I noticed quite a few big branches down on my way over here."

"Thanks, Poppa."

A few minutes later, Melody held her breath as she and Poppa went in through the silent gate.

"Oh, no!" she cried.

An enormous branch from one of the trees along the edge of the playground had split and fallen. It blocked two of the three handball courts. "I'll find someone to help move that," Poppa said.

But that was just one part of the playground. The rest was littered with twigs and leaves. Most of the geraniums had lost their clusters of red petals, and the bare stems were bent low. The morning glory vines had blown completely off the swing supports and were trailing on the ground. The green-bean tepees in the vegetable garden had toppled over. The hopscotch grids had washed away in the storm.

"Poppa, it's ruined!" Melody moaned. "We can't possibly fix all this before the picnic! What will we do?"

Poppa patted Melody's shoulder. "Nature fixes itself, Little One. You clean up as best you can, and then you wait. Wait for sun, wait for the strong roots of these plants to keep growing down under the earth. They're anchored, remember? And as long as those roots remain strong, they will continue to grow."

Melody was discouraged. "We were all done, Poppa,"

she sighed.

"A garden is never finished," Poppa said gently. "Gardens—and good works—keep going, but they both need tending. Keep tending the garden. Keep contributing to your community. Keep going."

Melody went home to think. Yvonne had told her to trust the people she was working with. So she called Diane and told her about the park. "I need help," Melody said.

"We need hands!" Diane said. "Let me call around. I'll call you back." She clicked off.

Melody called Val, Sharon, and Julius, and they all said the same thing: "I'll be right over."

A short time later, Melody and the others stood looking at the mess.

"Man!" Julius whistled. "It sure looks like a tornado hit! Look at that branch on the handball court!"

"You mean it's on the new brick wall?" Melody said.

Julius scrambled through the leaves. "Yeah! Knocked out some of the bricks, too."

Melody shook her head. "My grandfather is going to move the branch, but there's no way we can get the bricks fixed by Saturday."

"People can still play on the courts if we clear them out," Julius said.

Melody sighed. "Let's clean up the paths first."

"How can I help?" a voice behind them asked.

"Miss Esther!" Melody rushed to hug her. "Thank you for coming!"

"I'm here to work," Miss Esther said. "Where do you want me to start?"

Melody was about to answer when she saw a group of people appear at the gate. There were at least twenty kids from school and around the neighborhood. Some of them had rakes and brooms, and others carried garbage bags.

"What's going on?" Val asked.

"More hands," Diane said. "I asked a few people to help."

"Wow," Sharon whispered.

Melody smiled. "Okay," she said. "Let's keep going."

A Playground and a Party

CHAPTER 16

Melody could hardly believe it, but on Saturday, the playground was ready for a party. So many people had shown up to help on Thursday that all the branches and debris had been cleared from the paths. Most of the flowers had bounced back after a full Friday of sun. The morning glory vines hadn't survived the storm, so Melody and Miss Esther had trimmed them back. When Sharon had painted the fresh set of hopscotch grids on the path, she had surprised Melody by painting morning glories along the edges.

As she got dressed that morning, Melody looked at the wish list that she and Miss Esther had made as well as the plan for the playground that she had drawn. Both pieces of paper were taped to the wall above Melody's bed. The real playground didn't look exactly like the drawing, and there were things on the wish list that were still just wishes. But since Poppa had said that a garden is never finished, Melody decided that a playground never is either.

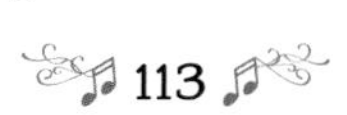

The Junior Block Club was meeting at the park at one o'clock to blow up the balloons that Poppa supplied for the party every year. At five minutes to one, Melody gathered her bags and called upstairs, "I'm going."

"We'll be there soon," Mommy called back down. "I've just got to pack up the food."

It was a perfect day to be outside. As soon as Melody got to the end of her block, she could see where the street had been blocked off. Neighbors were setting up card tables and lawn chairs in the road and putting coolers in the shade.

When she got to the park, Julius was standing at the gate, wearing a new striped T-shirt.

"Hey," he said, taking one of the bags from Melody.

"Hey, Julius." Melody grinned. "Thanks."

A minute later, Sharon came running from one direction while Diane arrived from the other. Val showed up with her mom. "We brought string for the balloons," Val called.

The group headed into the park, and Melody was happy to see that the playground was already busy. Some girls were playing jacks near the morning glory hopscotch paths, and a father was helping his little boy on the jungle gym. Kids were zipping down the slide and then running back to the ladder to take another turn.

Dwayne and his bandmates were setting up a mini stage next to the handball courts. There were big speakers and a couple of microphones. "What do you think of the setup?" Dwayne asked. "We recorded the instrumentals last night, but we'll be singing live today."

"This is great," she said. "I'm really glad you're here."

"You didn't think I'd miss this, did you?" Dwayne tugged at Melody's braid. She grinned and hurried back to her friends. Sharon and Julius were blowing up the balloons. Tish was cutting lengths of string from a spool, and Val and Diane were tying them to the balloons.

Melody took a big bunch of balloons to the front of the park and was tying them to the gate when Miss Esther made her way across the street. "Hello there, Melody," she called. "I see everything is in fine bloom, thanks to you!"

"Thanks to all of us," Melody said.

The park and the street in front of it began to fill, and soon it seemed as though the whole neighborhood was outside. Poppa and Big Momma and all the parents of the Junior Block Club members arrived at the playground at the same time.

"We want to take a picture of you five," Sharon's mother said. "We're so proud of all you've done."

At that moment, Dwayne spoke into a microphone. "Hello, neighbors," he said. "How about a hand for the

Junior Block Club that worked so hard to clean up our park!" When the kids were all up onstage, Dwayne introduced them each by name. The crowd hooted and cheered, and all the moms took out cameras.

"Over here," Mommy said.

"Look this way," Diane's mother called.

"I thought you said *a* picture," Sharon sighed.

"Hey, who is that?" Julius asked, pointing.

Melody saw a glamorous-looking lady step through the park gate, nodding and waving to the crowd.

"Who *is* that?" Melody asked.

"I know!" Diane said. "It's Martha Jean the Queen, from WCHB radio."

Melody couldn't believe it. Lots of people had contacted the Parks Department about their playground because they'd heard about it on Martha Jean's radio show. And all the phone calls and letters were what had prompted the Parks Department to take off the padlock. But Melody had never expected Miss Martha Jean to come to the park's grand opening. How did she even know about it?

"Look!" Melody whispered. Martha Jean was heading straight for the stage.

"Ladies and gentlemen," Dwayne said into the microphone. "It looks like we have a special guest. Miss Martha Jean Steinberg, the Queen of Detroit radio!"

Everyone applauded. Miss Martha Jean smiled for Tish's flashing camera before she strode across the stage in her high heels to stand next to Dwayne.

"God bless you and I love you," Miss Martha Jean said. Then she called out, "Melody Ellison?"

Melody's eyes grew wide. Dwayne motioned her over to the microphone. "Yes, ma'am?" Melody said, standing between her brother and Miss Martha Jean.

"So you're the young lady who wrote me about the playground project! Well, Melody, I came here today in person to congratulate you on your persistence, your dedication to your community, and . . ." she glanced around, "your hard work!" The crowd clapped again.

"Th . . . thank you," Melody said.

"And I have a proclamation to read from our mayor, the Honorable Jerome Cavanagh."

"The mayor?" Melody gasped.

Martha Jean nodded. She held up what looked like a picture frame with a letter under the glass. "Dear Miss Ellison," the Queen's radio voice rang out. "On behalf of the City of Detroit, we thank you and the Junior Block Club for your service to the community, and hereby officially reopen the Junior Block Club Children's Park and Playground!"

Melody was stunned. The park had been named for the

Junior Block Club! And the mayor knew her name! Melody heard the audience clapping as the other Junior Block Club members and their parents hooted and stomped.

"Thank you, Miss Queen," Melody said. "I mean, Miss The Queen . . . I mean . . ." She blinked and focused on the faces of her family.

Martha Jean patted her shoulder and laughed. "I think we should thank Melody for changing this park and playground into a beautiful place for all of us, and for being responsible enough to see it through!"

Now everyone began to cheer. Melody felt overwhelmed, but there was something important that she needed to say. She leaned into the microphone.

"Thank you," Melody said. She waited for the crowd to quiet. "But I didn't do this all myself. The playground changes only got done because lots of people made suggestions and gave advice." Melody looked at Poppa and Miss Esther, who were standing with Melody's parents. "And lots of people did the work." Melody waved the rest of the Junior Block Club over to stand by her. "There were also lots of neighborhood kids who helped, so thank you to them, too."

Everyone cheered again, and Tish took more pictures.

"Well, there's one more thing, Miss Ellison," Martha Jean said. "Since we got so many calls and pledges of

"Thank you," Melody said. "But I didn't do this all myself."

support at the station, I would like to present to the Junior Block Club this check for seventy-five dollars, to cover some of the cost of getting new swings for your playground. Congratulations, and please continue your good work, all of you! God bless you and I love you."

Melody was so full of feelings that she couldn't respond with words, so she hugged Miss Martha Jean to thank her. Then she took the check and filed off the stage with the rest of her friends.

Martha Jean stayed at the microphone and introduced Dwayne's group. "And now, our neighborhood Motown stars, The Three Ravens, will perform a song that's destined to be a hit."

The Queen suddenly stopped talking, and Melody turned back toward the stage to see why.

Dwayne had taken the microphone. "I'd like to ask my sister to come back up here," he said, motioning to Melody.

Melody's eyes met Dwayne's. "Me?" she mouthed.

Dwayne nodded. The music began and the audience went wild.

Melody stood still for a moment, smiling. Then she walked back to the stage along the hopscotch path, past some of the daylilies, past her parents' and grandparents' proud faces.

She thought about how hard Dwayne had worked to

make his record, how hard Lila always studied, and about the hard work Yvonne and so many others were doing to help justice and equality grow.

As she took a spot onstage beside her brother, Melody realized that her little idea of fixing up the playground had grown into something bigger and more beautiful than she'd ever imagined. She began to bounce happily to the music, raising her voice to sing with Dwayne. Melody knew the lyrics by heart, but today, they meant something different to her.

It's time for me to shine,
Make the jump to the big time.
Hit the road at a run,
Dance and jump and have some fun.
You know what that's gotta mean?
Girl, it's time that I move,
Time for movin' on up.

Melody knew in her heart that she would always remember this song, this place, and this day.

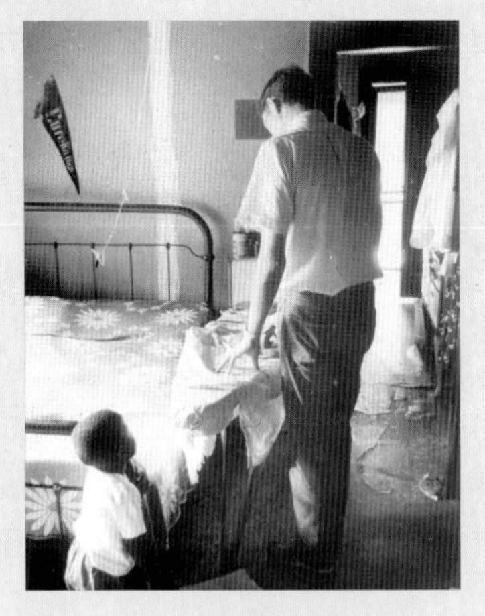

Freedom Summer workers stayed with local black families.

for kids. Like Melody's sister Yvonne, Freedom Summer volunteers went door-to-door inviting children of all ages to Freedom Schools. For many African American residents, it was the first time they had spoken to a white person. One black woman said, "Here, no white educated people talked to us." She commented that the white students "were just like anyone else."

Freedom School classes took place on front porches,

Almost all of the Freedom Schools published a student newspaper. Children got a chance to write their own poetry and plays, too.

College students taught classes to adults as well as children.

under trees, and in church basements. Like Yvonne, most of the college students had never taught before. But they were eager to help the kids learn how to read, write, and do math. They led classes in black history, the civil rights movement, and leadership skills. At night, the college students led classes for adults.

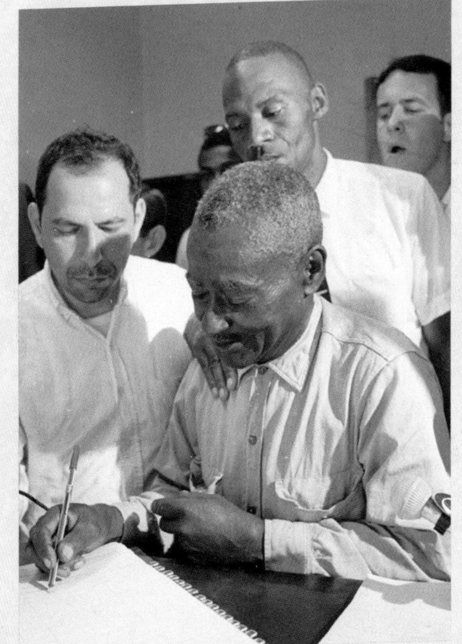

A 68-year-old man in Mississippi registered to vote for the first time.

Melody was proud of her sister for joining Freedom Summer. But she was worried about her, too. Volunteers were harassed and arrested and faced violence. Two white workers, Michael Schwerner and

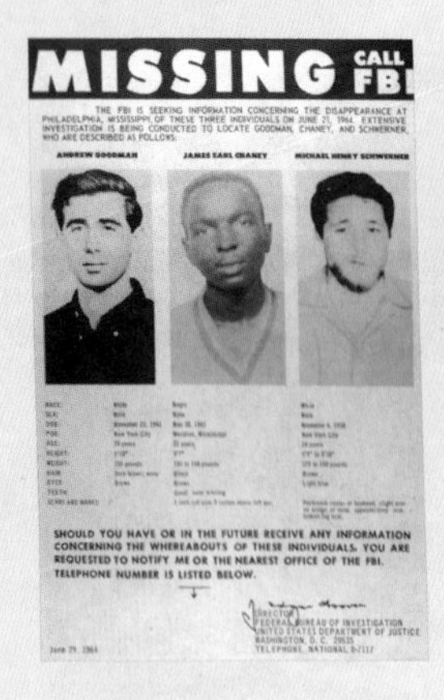

A poster of the missing civil rights workers and an image of their burned station wagon

Andrew Goodman, and a local African American man, James Chaney, disappeared on June 21. Their bodies were found on August 4. All three had been shot. It took 41 years before a member of the Ku Klux Klan, a violent hate group, was found guilty of killing the civil rights activists.

As Freedom Summer began, an important bill was signed into law. On July 2, 1964, the Civil Rights Act made segregation in public places illegal in every part of the country. Restaurants, movie theaters, parks, hotels, and stores could no longer refuse to serve black people, make them sit in separate sections, or use separate entrances. Although the law was passed, change did not happen overnight. It took months, and even years, before some public places provided black people with equal service.

The civil rights movement continues today. Americans have made great progress by ending legal segregation, but many people still face discrimination because of the color

This photo from the 1970s shows black children and white children attending the same school and drinking out of the same water fountains.

of their skin. People of all races—and all ages—continue to speak up and take action to make justice, equality, and dignity grow.

A New York City rally celebrating the 40th anniversary of Freedom Summer

Find more stories about these American Girl characters at bookstores and at AmericanGirl.com:

a Nez Perce girl who loves daring adventures on horseback

a Jewish girl with a secret ambition to be an actress

who joins the war effort when Hawaii is attacked

whose big ideas get her into trouble—but also save the day

who finds the strength to lift her voice for those who can't

who fights for the right to play on the boys' basketball team